S

Romantic & Sex
2 books in 1

Romantic and Sex and Eroticism Stories Between Nuns and Priests, of Love & Play Games Between the Parties

Written by:
Skye Jenkins

Immoral Tale

Stories of Sex and Eroticism Between Nuns and Priests, of Love & Play Games Between the Parties, and Much More

Written by:
Skye Jenkins

Table of Contents

Introduction

Immoral tales are the fabric of our culture. We read them in novels, watch them in movies, and listen to them on the radio. The term immoral story was first used by Elizabeth Kantor in her landmark book *The Immoral Tales: Forbidden Narratives from Around the World,* published in 1988. Kantor analyzed how different cultures use these stories to explore social issues like slavery, colonialism, women's oppression, masculinity.

The topics that are covered by immoral tales reflect all kinds of human experiences. Throughout history, people have used immoral stories to discuss the limits of what is considered acceptable behavior. Everything from fetishism, ritual murder, shamanic initiation, cannibalism, and prostitution is fair game. These stories are usually created in societies where "the society is faced with a dilemma. Either they must allow certain things to go on, or they must put an end to them. "These stories also show the evolution of moral standards in cultures and the crimes committed by individuals.

Although these stories are often violent and shocking, they can be used for good teaching and to create positive change within communities.

Immoral stories appeal to certain people because they provide more context and story, and you can use your imagination to make them work for you.

People are constantly debating whether or not pornography is healthy, and erotica is subjected to the same scrutiny. There's nothing wrong with reading erotica, and you'll get a lot more out of it than just pleasure. Here are a few of the countless benefits it provides.

Horror movies are possibly the most popular genre, but even genres like mysteries and science fiction use these themes. As you watch an immoral tale, you will see criminals being characterized by their victims. They see the victim as weak and can take advantage of that. In "The Torture Story", the witch is seen as a victim rather than a criminal. The witch is portrayed in this story as someone who is tricked into doing things that she does not want to do. The man and his family do not see her as a criminal but as someone who deserves what she gets.

About sex, it seems like there are no limits when it comes to immorality because of the stories that we talk about sex. Sex is something that we all have been taught to feel embarrassed about at some point in our lives. As children, we are told by our parents and teachers not to talk about sex and to never think of it. We are taught that sex should be saved for those special people in our lives, like our spouse or significant other. Immorality as related to sex is seen through different perspectives, such as male dominance and female submission.

It is also important to remember that these stories can be very graphic and show us what people are capable of doing, whether physically or mentally. "Immoral stories take the broadest perspectives-long, panoramic sweeps through time, across cultures." By taking a broad approach, readers can see what happens when a person commits immoral actions and what other events occur because of those actions.

A Priest Goes Bad

As the sun's rays began to trickle in through the blinds, Father Matthew awakened.

As the entire weight of last night's adventure brought him down, he collapsed back into his bed. He thought it might have been a dream for a brief period, but the realism of the pictures and sensations rapidly disproved that theory. It had occurred. He felt a shudder run down his spine. He'd succumbed to the same temptations that had brought him to this point in the first place. He'd arrived for his first posting as a newly ordained priest the day before. He wondered what the future held as he glanced at the ceiling above him.

He couldn't bring himself to blame Emma, Sister Catherine, or whatever her name was. He understood his flaws and inadequacies were entirely his own. Emma had reawakened a passion that had been lying dormant for a long time. That was clear to him now. It would have been someone else, sometime else, if it hadn't been Emma.

Nonetheless, it was difficult to deny that she had a peculiar hold on him. He questioned if he would have given in to anyone. After all, Emma stood out among his countless conquests; she was different from the rest.

Father Murray, the eldest of the two, responded, "Welcome." "I was told that one of our nuns had already shown you around the place."

He replied, "Yes." "By Em—" says the narrator. He swallowed his saliva as he realized what he had almost done. "By Sister Catherine—" says the narrator.

The priest smiled and nodded. "Excellent. I'm sure she answered all of your questions regarding the church and its history. She is meticulous."

Matt was on the verge of choking on his coffee. His face flushed scarlet with that phrase: "very thorough." He felt positive that Father Murray was unaware of the full extent of the situation.

—"Yes, yes, yes. She was quite beneficial." Though he had managed to keep the images of his immoral night at bay until that point, they returned with a vengeance now. Matt's mind wandered back to the previous night. He felt the urge to see Emma's building quickly as

Father Murray droned on about duties—which masses he would be in charge of, how they divided weddings and funerals when confessions were held, and which feast days necessitated special masses for the students at the adjoining school.

When breakfast was completed, he was relieved to be able to sneak away to his room. After closing the door, he sank to his knees and prayed to the Lord, begging for forgiveness as well as courage and resolve to overcome the temptations that had suddenly awakened inside him. As he fingered the beads of his rosary and prayed to the Holy Spirit for redemption, he bent his head and fell into a deep trance.

His fears of a constant barrage of temptation were proven to be unfounded after that first day and night. Emma was a rare sight for him, and he only saw her in passing. Although the nuns shared the rectory, dividers had been created to ensure that the two groups did not have any common contact within the structure. He only encountered the source of his temptation in the church or at school. He murmured a silent prayer of appreciation that they were in a public location at that time.

The relief he had felt at first began to fade as he settled into a routine. He meditated on the subject for a long time in his head, hoping for insight to help him find out what was bothering him. But no answer appeared to come, or at least not one that made any sense, no matter how long he prayed. While he had initially thanked God each morning when he awoke to see that Emma had not attempted to recreate their first-midnight encounter, he now began to fantasize about a repeat. He awoke each morning with the acute sting of disappointment, despite his reluctance to admit it to himself.

Disappointment barely lasted a few moments before shame took its place. Then, he dragged himself from bed to the chapel, where he spent his first waking hour in prayer that offered no relief.

After that first night with Emily, he carried on like that for nearly five weeks before he had the chance to revisit it. On a Saturday morning, he heard confessions. There had been a continuous stream of penitents all morning, but as the afternoon wore on, the line had thinned to just a few. As another individual entered the booth on the opposite side of the wall, he became tired and hungry. The voice's recognizability jolted him back to consciousness.

—"Bless me, father, for I have sinned," Emma replied, her voice unmistakable. As desire rose in him, he felt a cold sweat break out on his forehead. The remarks had a seductive edge to them, which he knew was deliberate.

—"Tell me your sins, my child," he forced the words out robotically, trying to get a grip on the pulsing arousal that flooded through his body and mind.

—"I have been short with my colleagues," she began innocently enough. "I have neglected my duties on occasion. And I have not always given all of my energy in the service of the Lord."

—"None of us is perfect," Matt said, his voice shaking. "It is important that you acknowledge your shortcomings, however, so that God can forgive you and give you new strength in the future."

—"But I have done other things," whispered Emma, barely loud enough for him to hear it. "And I am not sure they can be so easily forgiven."

He could not help himself. He knew what those things were. He knew where this would lead, and yet something in his mind

overruled those parts of his mind, and he had no choice but to continue.

—"The Lord is forgiving and merciful. Tell me your sins and be free of the guilt." He waited breathlessly for her response. The silence was almost unbearable for him as he struggled to control the radiating excitement through his body.

—"I have been a naughty little nun."

Her word pierced his defenses, and he let out a soft moan. He could feel himself beginning to grow hard as she continued her 'confession.'

—"I do my best to live by the codes of my order, but sometimes the pleasures of flesh call out to me more strongly than I can resist. I lust after so many people that I see: men and women alike. And no matter how hard I try, I find it impossible to resist these urges. No matter what I do, I am overmatched by the need for physical release. I have done unspeakable things with my fellow nuns. I have explored their bodies, and they have explored mine. We have given into all kinds of depravity, and we have resisted no impulse of our body."

His breathing was heavy now as he listened to her recount her sins. The blood flowed quickly into his member now, and he was nearly fully erect. He knew that his body would soon be begging for release. Though he knew better, he could not help himself. His hand fell to the bulge in his pants, and he began to rub himself as he urged her to continue.

—"Is that all?"

—"No, Father McMillan." He felt a surge of lust go through him at the way she said his name.

—"I took my lust even further," she said. "I'm afraid that I have gone too far to be forgiven. Not only have I engaged in evil with the other nuns, all of whom were ready and able, I also corrupted another of God's servants, one who was walking a righteous path before I tempted him."

His mouth was dry now, and each time his hand moved over his erection, he was forced to stifle a moan.

—"Well, that is quite serious, Sister. The Lord forgives, but you must confess fully to be forgiven."

His heart hammered in his chest. He knew this was wrong, perhaps even worse than the first time. Not only was he indulging his own lust, but he was profaning a sacrament to do it. But all of that faded into the background, entirely overwhelmed by the lust.

—"He was a new priest, fresh from the seminary. When I saw his name, I was reminded of my past life. We had gone to college together, and I had seduced him once. I barged into his room and disrobed immediately. I took his cock and made it mine. I sucked him dry once, and then I brought him back to full attention before I hopped on and rode him until he burst again.

—"Thoughts of that day filled my mind, and I knew even before I saw him again that I would have to have him. And I did not miss my opportunity. I snuck into his room the first night he was here and gave him the same pleasure I gave him all those years ago. I stroked his raging cock as he moaned and trembled, and I was rewarded as he blew his load in my mouth and all over my face and tits. It was entirely and completely wrong, but I had never experienced anything hotter."

His hand shook. His cock ached. He could hardly form thoughts through the lust that clouded his mind. He needed her now, even

worse than he had that first night. An idea struck him, as wrong as it was arousing, and without a thought to the divine punishment that would await him, he chose to enact it.

—"These are serious crimes, Sister Catherine." He used her name even though the confession was ostensibly anonymous. "And only serious penance can save your soul now."

—"That was what I was worried about," she said in a deep whisper. "Tell me what I need to do. I will do anything you command."

His hand shook as he reached up toward the slidable partition. His finger closed around the wooden knob, and he slid back the screen. He was face to face with Emma now. She pouted at him, her big doe-eyes looking at him with a level of innocence he was sure she did not possess.

—"What is my punishment, Father McMillan?" She asked, her voice soft and girlish. "I will submit to any punishment you require."

—"Well," he said, expending a great deal of effort to keep his voice from shaking as he spoke, "as a nun, chastity is your vow. Your

sexuality is not yours to give; it belongs to the Lord. Remember, though our God is merciful, he is also a vengeful and jealous God. He does not kindly take when others give and take what rightly belongs to him. It seems only fair that those things you have given away must now be given back to the Lord. As his representative here on earth, I will receive them on his behalf."

He paused as he let his words sink in. A delighted smile spread across Emma's face, and he knew that she appreciated the game that he had concocted. Outside of the church, he was a mere mortal and what they had done was wrong, but in here, he was the representative of God, and in that role, he could balance out the other sins they had committed and, in so doing, experience twice the pleasure.

He stood so that his waist was even with the upper edge of the window between the two booths. The bulge in his khaki pants was unmistakable, and he imagined Emma's look as she now came face to face with it.

—"The debt cannot just be repaid one for one," he said softly. The confessionals were designed not to allow sound out, but he still felt on edge knowing that other people were waiting just outside. "The

Lord demands more to make right for the wrong you have done him."

—"Of course, Father McMillan. That only seems fair. What does the lord command?"

Her voice was so innocent; she played the role perfectly, much to Matt's delight. In the rectory, she had taken control, but here, she was the submissive nun, and he was the priest, possessed of all the authority of his office.

—"I believe that oral penance is the only way to make up for your crimes."

He paused for a moment as he waited for a response. All he heard from the other side was a low moan. He decided to take the authority angle one step further.

—"Sister Catherine," he said in an emphatic whisper. "I have given you your penance. I expect you to begin immediately."

—"Of course, Father. Forgive me." Her answer was quick and apologetic.

Matt felt his arousal rising as he fell deeper into the role.

He gasped as he felt her hands close around his bulge. She teased him for only a moment before she undid the belt, unzipped the pants, and fished his aching cock out from his boxers. He shuddered as he felt her fingers brush against his naked skin. His mind went blank with lust as he felt the heat of her breath. A moment later, he nearly fainted as her warm, wet mouth enveloped his pulsing cock.

He was forced to brace himself to keep his legs steady as Sister Catherine went from zero to sixty in seconds. She didn't waste any time building him up. Instead, she began bobbing up and down, noisily slobbering on his cock with such enthusiasm that Matt was worried he was going to pop right there.

He bit down on his closed fist as he braced himself against the insane pleasure that was filling him at the moment. Looking down, he could see nothing but one of Emma's hands as it fondled his balls. The fact that he couldn't see her as she sucked him off only made it hotter. The act was so forbidden, so absolutely taboo, and yet he was doing it. Only a handful of weeks ago, as he prepared to come to his first Parish, he would never have imagined this. It simply wasn't possible. And yet, as the pleasure built and built inside of him, he

said a silent prayer, this time in thanks for the opportunity to experience such incredible pleasure.

She expertly worked his cock, forcing him to marvel at just how good a blowjob could feel. Her lips slid up and down his shaft as her tongue darted and swirled around it. Every once in a while, she would pause as she reached the bottom, and taking a deep breath, she would force his cock even deeper down into her throat, gagging herself for a few seconds before coming up for air. The whole world seemed to be spinning, and he knew that he would not be able to hold out much longer.

—"Oh, God," he moaned. "Oh, Sister Catherine. Oh God, yes!"

She added both hands to the mix, using one to stroke his shaft as her tongue assaulted his swollen head, and her other hand coaxed the cum from his balls. After only a few seconds of this new approach, he exploded. He could feel the force of his orgasm as the cum shot out in thick, powerful jets, filling Sister Catherine's mouth. His knees went weak, and he had to support himself with both hands against the wall to stop from falling. His vision became blurry as lightheaded pleasure assaulted him with fury. So intense was the pleasure that it seemed like no other part of his body could function properly.

As he finally managed to come down, he slowed his ragged breathing, fearful that someone else might hear. Sister Catherine released his cock from her mouth, but not before she sucked dry every last bit of cum. Too overcome by exhaustion, Matt collapsed into a seated position and rested his hands on his knees. He raised his head, and his eyes met with Sister Catherine's. He nearly fainted as he saw her: her mouth was open with a pool of his cum filling it. She closed her mouth and swallowed, moaning in delight. Then she licked her lips and smiled at him. She leaned in close, her face framed by the window.

—"Thank you so much, Father," she said. "I hope the Lord is satisfied."

He was too stunned to respond. She winked at him and giggled like a schoolgirl, closing the partition before exiting the confessional.

A Priest Goes Bad 2

With two unforgivable transgressions, Matt expected to be overwhelmed by his guilt. Instead, he found himself oddly at peace, which in its way was unsettling. He expected, maybe in some sense even wanted, to feel shame and guilt, to feel as if he had done something wrong, and yet as he continued to reminisce about that day in the confessional and that night in his room. As he imagined a dozen other scenarios not yet come to pass, he couldn't help but be filled with silent contentment that baffled his conscious mind.

In the manner as before, he found that he rarely saw for the next few weeks after his encounter with Emma. He kept hoping that she would surprise him in his room or present herself for another confession, but she did not. And he began to grow restless, even as the memories of their times together filled him with warmth. He knew, though, that such memories were not enough. She had awakened a hunger in him that he could hardly keep at bay, and he feared that his newfound peace of mind would not last if he were forced to bottle up all his passions in such a way.

With that in mind, he slowly made up his mind that if Emma were not going to come to him, he would have to go to her. It was the only logical choice to be made in the situation—if the choice to sneak through the rectory at night to make it to the nun's chambers to possibly engage in sexual activities with one of the sisters could ever be considered a logical thing for a priest to do. Such concerns, however, did not register on Father McMillan's mind as he stalked through the darkened hallways of the rectory just a little bit after midnight. He knew that getting caught would put him in an awkward spot, but he was not worried. After all, even in their wildest dreams, he doubted any of the other priests could imagine what he was setting out to do.

A temporary wall had partitioned off the section of the rectory that the nuns stayed in, but seeing as how it wasn't exactly Fort Knox, there was no lock on the door that divided the two genders from one another. Matt quietly turned the handle, bit by bit, until he could silently push open the door. Inside, he had no way of knowing which room was Emma's, but he had a hunch that it might not be all that difficult to find. Earlier in the day, he had seen Emma giggling with one of the other young nuns, whose name Matt did not know. From the looks on their faces, he had a feeling they weren't just exchanging

innocent little jokes. Perhaps tonight was one of the nights that Emma engaged in activities with details she had tantalized Matt.

He stopped at the first door and turned his ear to face it. Waiting silently, he counted to ten before moving on to the next one and then the next. By the time he reached the last door (there were only five), he could feel his disappointment. Perhaps, his plan was not going to work. Resigned that he would likely have to head back to his own room and take care of matters himself, Matt turned his ear to the door once more and listened. He counted... one... two... three... by the time he reached nine, he was already ready to leave, but then he heard it: a little giggle followed by a soft moan. His heart was in his throat as he listened. Another moan, and then another, clearly from two different people: his plan had worked. Steeling himself for what was about to happen, he paused, took a deep breath, and then knocked softly on the door.

On the other side, the moans ceased immediately. Five seconds of silence were followed by nervous whispers and the movement of the sounds on the other side. He heard footsteps approaching the door, and a moment later, it opened.

Sister Catherine smiled at him. —"Father McMillan, what a pleasant surprise. Why don't you come in?"

She opened the door wider and stepped aside to allow the priest's entrance. Once inside, he stopped in his tracks and spotted the nun he had seen earlier gossiping with Sister Catherine. Her bare shoulder peeked out from underneath the thin bedsheet that she had wrapped tightly around her midsection. He gulped as he looked her up and down, admiring the swell of her breasts as they pressed against the sheet.

—"Good evening, Father," she said in a sultry tone. As he looked at her, he didn't doubt that Emma had let slip the secret of their rendezvous. He could see the lust in her eyes, and he felt himself growing aroused at the thought.

—"This is Sister Maria," Emma said.

Sister Maria was shorter than Emma, and though he could tell that she was not as slim as Emma, her curves more than made up for it. Even though the gossiping sheet, he could tell that her tits were massive. Emma's were a good size, C's maybe, but Maria's were DD's at least, maybe even EE's.

—"A pleasure to meet you," he said, as his eyes devoured her form. He tried to imagine what she must have looked like naked, and he could not help but stiffen at the thought.

—"What brings you here tonight, Father McMillan?" Emma asked in a voice that was all business.

Matt froze. He had spent so much energy deliberating on whether or not even to come that he genuinely hadn't given much thought as to what he was going to do once he got here. Luckily, Emma was always quick on her feet.

—"It must be that discipline issue that I spoke to you about earlier," she said, her tone leading him toward agreement. She looked at the other nun. "About Sister Maria, no? She has been quite a bad little nun lately, and I think she needs some punishment."

He took the ball and ran with it. He shifted his gaze to Sister Maria and nodded sternly. "Yes, of course. I have come to give some discipline to you, Sister. I am afraid that your transgressions have brought you into sin, and we simply must do something about it." He waited for a moment, nervously wondering if Sister Maria would be up for their little game.

—"I am so sorry, Father McMillan," she said, fighting back a smile. She sat up and released her grip on the sheets. The swell of her breasts was enough to keep it in place, but Matt could hardly breathe as he waited to see if it would fall. When it didn't, he decided that he would have to take control of things. He crossed the room quickly and, in one motion, pulled back the sheet to reveal the curvy nun in all her glory.

He felt the blood pour into his cock as he drank in her beautiful naked body. Her heavy tits were graced with beautiful dark nipples that drove him wild. He wanted nothing more than to lean down at taking them into his mouth, but his eyes continued to wander, and that thought was pushed from his head.

—"Turn over," he commanded, his voice gaining authority as the game went along.

She complied without hesitation, and he sucked in his breath at sight. Her plump ass rose like a perfect bubble. His erection was becoming painful now as he stepped up to the bed.

—"Hands and knees," he barked.

Again, Sister Maria followed his orders without a second thought. He cast a glance over at Sister Catherine, who only smiled knowingly back at him. He imagined that she had already taught Maria the importance of following orders. Turning his gaze back to the naked nun, he felt his breath catch. In this position, both her massive tits and her curvy ass were on full display for him.

He leaned down so that his mouth was only a few inches from her ear. "You have been a naughty nun, Sister Maria, and now I must punish you."

Drawing back his hand, he paused for a moment and locked eyes with the patiently waiting nun. There was nothing there but lust. He brought down his hand forcefully against her ass, admiring the way her flesh jiggled from the impact. She cried out at the force. He drew back his hand and smacked her ass again, eliciting a noise that was half-whimper, half-moan.

—"Oh, yes," she said as he brought down his hand the third time. "I have been bad."

—"Shhh." He brought one finger to his lip. "If the others hear you, Sister Maria, you will be in even more trouble. You must be silent."

He could see that the idea of having to keep quiet only excited her more. She wiggled her hips in delight as he smacked her again and again. She shifted to her elbows so that she could bury her face in the pillow in front of her, which was the only way to muffle her screams.

Her ass cheeks reddened from his disciplinary actions, and he decided that she had been punished enough. He paused his spanking, but Maria's face was still buried in the pillow, as her body still trembled with pleasure. He moved his hands lower than his previous target and brushed his fingertips against the outer lips of Sister Maria's soaking pussy. Her whole body tensed up for a moment as she unleashed a muffled scream that he could hear even though the pillow's sound was dampening.

—"You have been punished enough, Sister Maria," he said. "Now, it is time for your reward."

She raised her head and looked at him. Her face was flushed and her eyes wild with passion. Her mouth hung open as she sucked in deep breaths to try to calm the sexual excitement that was coursing through her.

—"Off the bed," he commanded. "On your knees in front of me."

She scrambled off the bed excitedly, assuming the position she was commanded to take. He looked down at her and felt his cock twitch. He was aching for release, and now he would find it.

—"Touch yourself," he said as his own hands began to undo his belt. He stripped his lower half down to nothing as Sister Maria's fingers moved frantically over her clit. Her eyes were glued to his cock as it was finally free from its cage. Her mouth hung open, and Matt could see the hunger.

"Spit on it," he said, and Maria went immediately to work. She grabbed his pulsing shaft with her free hand and began to coat it with her saliva.

—"Wait," Sister Catherine interrupted.

Matt looked over to see her bringing an unmarked plastic bottle. She smiled wickedly at him as she tipped the bottle and poured body oil all over his cock and Maria's juicy tits.

—"I think that is what you were going for, no?"

The devilish look in her eyes drove Matt crazy, and she was exactly right. He was going to fuck those big beautiful tits, and now with this new lubricant, it was going to be even better.

—"Push your tits together, Sister Maria."

Their already ridiculous size would have been comical as she pushed them together were it not for how incredibly sexy she looked down on her knees, holding her oiled-up tits and looking up at him with a needy pout. He stepped forward and used his hand to push his cock into those pillowy folds. He let out a sigh as their warmth engulfed his prick. He locked eyes with Maria and began to thrust.

Almost immediately, he realized that he would not last long. The buildup of the last few weeks, coupled with the spanking, had him ready to blow. That was fine with him, however. Now that he was here in Sister Catherine's room going to town on another nun's rack, he was sure that things were going to be different. No longer would he wait weeks between encounters. No, it was going to be much more frequent.

Sister Catherine, who had been watching from the sideline up to that point, decided to get involved. Still clothed in her rather skimpy

robe, she knelt beside Maria and used her hands to pick up Maria's left off.

The busty nun shook as Sister Catherine played with her pussy. She let out a whimper and closed her eyes as the other nun's skillful hands brought her closer to release. Matt could tell from her face that she enjoyed it and that she wasn't going to last very long like him.

His thrusting picked up speed as he neared his finish. He felt a familiar sensation building in his balls as his cock pounded Maria's beautiful cleavage. His vision went blurry, and his knees grew weak.

—"Oh fuck," he hissed through his clenched teeth. "Here it comes!"

That announcement seemed to set Maria off as well. She threw her head back just as the priest's cock began to explode. Matt watched in awe as ropes of his cum fired up, hitting her neck and chest, before sliding back down to cover her massive tits. Maria bit her lips as Catherine continued to play with her clit. Her body tensed and shook, and she whimpered for half a minute before she collapsed from a combination of pleasure and exhaustion.

Matt, with his pants still around his ankles, looked down at the two nuns. Smiling, he pulled back up his pants and quickly buckled his belt.

—"Very good, sisters. I hope to see both of you in confession."

The Six Priests and a Nun

There had been difficult moments in the past, with drugs and desire, as well as more than a few run-ins with the law, but that was more than a half-decade ago. She had repented, confessed her sins, and dedicated herself to the Lord's service. Whatever transgressions she had made, she had been forgiven and forgotten. Until last night, her soul was pure and purified, and she was ready to join the Almighty Father in paradise.

She couldn't figure out what had happened no matter how many times she replayed the events in her thoughts. Even though she knew it was wrong to go there, he had been so lovely and nice. He had done nothing wrong, except perhaps tempting her, she knew. After his mother's funeral, she accepted the offer. She was the one who had accepted the first glass of wine he gave, as well as the subsequent glasses. She hadn't objected; she hadn't refused when the act of comfort morphed into something more. Her words, as well as her body, had consented. It was something she had wished. That

was beyond a shadow of a question. There was no doubt that there would be a cost associated with it immediately.

Her fate was being decided just beyond the wooden door that stood in front of her. She couldn't decide whether to pray for mercy or whether this was a silly thought. She might get kicked out. It was a possibility, if not a foregone conclusion. What would she do then? When she arrived at the monastery, she had nothing and looked for hope in a terrible world. There was nowhere for her to go if she was kicked out.

The door opened after what seemed like a lifetime, and the abbess' harsh gaze met her own. Sister Roberta was long over retirement age, but she was defiant and refused to go while still running the convent's day-to-day operations. She had just celebrated eight and a half decades on our planet last month.

—"The priests will see you now, Sister Kelly."

Kelly followed the abbess into the sacristy, where he discovered six men clothed in ritual garb. The priests were clothed in their vestments, the clothes they wore to celebrate sacraments, rather than everyday life's regular black and white collared clothing.

Sister Roberta pushed her forward till she was standing in the middle of the half-circle made by the half dozen pastors. She shifted her gaze from guy to man, aware that they were in charge of her future. They looked in chronological order, with the youngest on the left and the oldest on the right. She couldn't have been much older than the priest on the far left. Her twenty-fifth birthday was coming up in less than a month.

The eldest priest said, "Sister Kelly." He was known to her as Monsignor Mark. He had been the parish priest for about a decade, including her time at the convent. "You understand why you're here." It wasn't a question at all. "Grave sins necessitate grave punishments. Sister Roberta came to us with your confessed misdeeds, and she made the right decision. Some situations are too sensitive or too startling for the abbess to address alone. As a result, I have summoned the priests of my Parish to debate this matter and render a judgment commensurate with your crime."

He took a breath and stopped. The words appeared to linger in the thick, stale air. Sister Kelly felt as if she couldn't catch her breath. She understood she would be expelled. She would have given anything to be able to undo her actions at that point, but she couldn't. She

needed the courage to face the repercussions of her actions right now. Her lips uttered a silent prayer.

Monsignor Mark spoke it again, "Sister Roberta, again, thank you for bringing this to our attention, but I believe it would be better if you waited outside until Sister Kelly and I had finished speaking."

Kelly saw the abbess's contented smile fade away. She had undoubtedly expected to be able to observe the events. Sister Roberta had always had a vicious streak to her as if she reveled in the punishments meted out to others.

Sister Robert walked away with a nod. Sister Kelly was the only witness in front of her jury.

The Monsignor responded, "You don't have to be so tense." "Things aren't as horrible as you think."

Kelly wanted to believe him, but she couldn't allow herself to rest until she had more proof.

—"You have two difficulties on your hands: the first is your misdeeds. Monsignor Mark went on to say, "The second is your misdeeds." "As for your sins, they are forgiven because of your

repentance. It is not our place to pass judgment on your flaws. We all make mistakes, and it is our responsibility to forgive and offer penance to the contrite. Following the conclusion of this meeting, one of the dads present will hear your confession, and the problem will be resolved."

—"However, the second issue is more important, and deciding on it is more difficult. We may forgive you as a parishioner, but it does not imply we can forgive you as a sister and church servant in your professional capacity. We must be held to a higher standard as shepherds for the Lord. It is for this reason that we take oaths. That is why we devote so much of our time to prayer. You have failed, you have betrayed the congregation's faith in you, and you have done it in the most flagrant way possible."

The Monsignor took a breather. Kelly began to tremble. The feeling of being unable to breathe was becoming increasingly severe. Her lungs appeared to be unwilling or unable to respond to the impulses supplied by her brain. She realized she was on the verge of a full-fledged panic attack.

Just when she thought she was going to lose it, she felt a hand on her shoulder. She turned to see the youngest priest smiling at her. He ran his hand down her back.

—"Calm, Sister Kelly. Calm," he said.

There was a true warmth in his smile and calmness in his tone and in his touch that melted her anxiety. She felt the tightness in her chest dissipate as her heart slowed its relentless beating. The priest patted her on the back when she could breathe normally again and resumed his place in the half-circle.

—"Thank you, Father Tyler," the Monsignor said. "Now, Sister Kelly, there are options. There is hope. We will not expel you from your post without giving you your chance at redemption. We cannot simply forgive and forget, but we believe in second chances. And, though a minor concern, you can imagine that the rumors your dismissal would create are not generally beneficial to the church. We certainly wouldn't want sisters within the convent finding out about your actions, the community at large even less so."

The Monsignor paused and smiled at her warmly. The smile gave her heart. Perhaps all was not lost. This man seemed genuinely concerned for her, genuinely willing to give her a second chance. His

was a face you could trust. Though nearing fifty, his skin was unblemished and what wrinkles he had only gave him a distinguished look. The same could be said for the streaks of gray that emanated from his temples. He had a strong jaw that lent authority to his appearance. As she looked at him, she realized that he was a man born to be a leader.

She smiled back at him. "Thank you, Monsignor. You have no idea how grateful I am."

His smile narrowed as he furrowed his brow. "Well, do not yet thank me, Sister. You have not yet heard your punishment."

There was an ominous sound in his voice, and suddenly, the comfort she had gained just a few moments ago vanished. She tried to calm herself. Her anxiety was simply getting the best of her. What could be worse than expulsion and disgrace? She would do what they asked: a hundred rosaries, a thousand Hail Mary's. She would clean the church from top to bottom with a toothbrush if that were what was needed.

—"Whatever you command of me, in your wisdom, I will accept as my just and deserved punishment."

The Monsignor nodded. "Very good. Very good. Your crimes are of a nature that dictates the nature of your punishment. A sin of the flesh deserves a punishment of the flesh."

Those words sent a chill through her. Indeed, he could not mean corporal punishment. Catholic sects practiced flagellation, but always as a self-imposed penance, never as a punishment from one person to another.

—"Do you know why what you did was a sin, Sister Kelly?" Monsignor Mark asked.

The question caught her off guard. She was not a theologian, but it seemed to her self-evident.

—"I broke my vows of chastity."

The priest nodded. "Yes, and why is it that nuns take vows of chastity?"

—"Like priests, we take them so that we can be pure in body and mind in our service to the Lord." It was the first answer that sprang to her mind, but as she saw the monsignor frown, she knew it was not what he was looking for.

—"Like priests?" He shook his head. "Nuns are not *like priests*, nor are their vows. Nuns take vows of celibacy as a way of giving themselves completely to the Lord. They belong to him, body and soul. By breaking your vow, you have not simply made yourself impure, but you have given something to a man that by rights belonged to God. Ours is a jealous God, Sister Kelly. Surely, you know your scripture. He is not pleased when others receive what is his by rights. To make it right, he must receive his due."

—"His due?" Sister Kelly asked. She was puzzled. What exactly was the Monsignor talking about?

—"What you have given to man must now be given to God. As his representatives here on earth, we six fathers stand as proxies for the Lord. We shall receive the payment due to the Almighty to redeem you for your transgressions."

Sister Kelly stared blankly as her mind began to comprehend the words "you cannot mean."

Monsignor Mark held up his hand. "I do mean it. You have a decision. Repay your debt or be expelled. Choose now."

Her mind spun. Her heart pounded. She felt her lungs gasp for air. Her hands trembled at her side. Shame washed over her as she thought of what she had done, of what she now had to do. She could not leave the order. She could not leave the church.

She bowed her head. —"I will do as you command."

—"Very good. You will begin with Father Tyler. Approach him."

She turned and walked toward the young priest. He stared back at her impassively, though she could see a bead of sweat sitting on his forehead. As she stopped before him, the Monsignor continued speaking.

"Since we cannot trust you to have given all the details of your acts, we must be thorough. There are six of us. With each, you shall perform an act as offering to the Lord so that no matter your sins with that man, the Lord will be repaid in full. To begin, you will give pleasure to Father Tyler with your hands. You may start."

She trembled as she sank to her knees. Father Tyler lifted his vestment over his head. Beneath, he wore only a white t-shirt and a pair of boxers. Kelly could already see the bulge straining against his underwear. She reached for the waistband and pulled it down,

revealing his manhood. It was six inches long. With each heartbeat, it seemed to pulse. She marveled at it. Taking it in her hand, she began to stroke it up and down.

This, she had not done with the grieving man. She felt a strange thrill at the thought of masturbating a man with her hand and a priest no less. She wondered if he had ever been touched like this by a woman before. By the look of pure ecstasy on Father Tyler's face, she guessed that he had not, or that, at least, it had been some time since he had. The priest's cock grew in her hand as she continued to stroke it. He grunted each time her fingers brushed against the swollen tip. She smiled up at him and continue to jack him off faster and faster.

—"Sister Kelly," he moaned. "Don't stop. I'm close."

The Six Priests and a Nun 2

The knowledge that this was a punishment seemed buried somewhere deep inside her mind, and she found herself encouraged by the priest's words. She quickened her pace as she felt him throb and pulse in her hand. She watched in wonder as his balls jerked up toward his body. A moment later, a blast of white goo fired from the head of his manhood. Her mouth was open in wonder, and the first jet landed on her tongue. The taste and the sensation surprised her, but she found that it was not unpleasant. She continued to stroke the spasming cock, and the next half dozen ropes of cum landed on her face and habit. When he was finished, she released his deflating cock from her hand, and Father Tyler let out a moan of contentment.

—**"Very good, Sister Kelly."**

She had lost herself in lust as she had brought the young priest to orgasm. The Monsignor's voice reminded her that five others had been her audience. She felt herself wetter at the thought.

—"Next is Father Williams," the priest informed her. The next man in line was only slightly older than Father Tyler, perhaps in his early thirties. His hair was a mop of curly blonde rings, and his eyes were blue and piercing. "Your mouth will be your next offer to our Lord."

Kelly did not need further instructions to understand that one. Father Williams shed his vestment, and his boxers followed after. Sister Kelly licked her lips as she stared at his fat cock. It was only slightly longer than Father Tylers, but it was near twice as thick. When she wrapped her hand around the shaft, she wasn't even able to touch her fingers together.

Her hands worked him quickly to his full length and hardness. She paused for a moment as she stared at the perimeter. This was going to be quite a difficult task, but she knew she was up for it. She licked her lips again, this time to lubricate them rather than simply in anticipation. Then she leaned her head forward and took the head of his cock into her mouth.

Her lips stretched around the massive girth. She could feel the muscles in her face and jaw straining as they were stretched nearly as far as they could go. She could hardly believe that she was doing this. Her jaw ached as she pushed his fat shaft deeper into her mouth.

Not only was she once again engaging in carnal acts, but this time it was with a room full of priests.

She gradually got used to the massive cock as it stretched her oral cavity. She increased her pace as the father muttered encouragement that was rather unpriestly.

—"Oh, fuck yes," he moaned as she buried almost his entire shaft into her mouth. "Suck my cock, you dirty fucking slut. Make me cum, Sister Kelly."

Hearing him speak that way while still using her title made her shudder with arousal. She was only too happy to continue to pleasure him and grant his wish. She had gotten her first taste of cum when she had jerked off Father Tyler, and now, she found herself hungering for more.

Father Williams's groans grew louder, and she knew she wouldn't have to wait much longer for her second taste. One of her free hands found his testicles, and she massaged them as she continued to bob up and down on his cock as quickly as she could. She could feel how swollen and heavy with cum his testicles were, and she wanted nothing more than to relieve the pressure… directly into her mouth. Soon enough, she got her wish.

Father Williams let out a loud moan, and she felt his testicles jump in her hand. An instant later, a flood of semen was firing out of his shaft. The first blast splashed against the roof of her mouth, but as she forced his spurting manhood deeper into her throat, he fired straight down her esophagus and into her stomach. He seemed to cum for a longer time than Father Tyler had. When he was finished, Sister Kelly could feel a load of cum sloshing in her stomach. She loved it.

—"Two down," Monsignor Mark announced. "And only four more to go. I must say you are doing quite a good job, Sister Kelly. I knew we were right to give you a chance at redemption."

Strangely, she felt herself swell with pride at the compliment. There was some part of that craved male approval; perhaps she had always craved it.

—"Next is Father Jack. Before we can continue, I would ask you to disrobe."

She obeyed without hesitation. She removed her head covering and quickly pulled her habit over her head. She was left in her bra and panties, which were nothing more than plain beige undergarments

she had purchased at a local discount store, not exactly sexy lingerie. It was no matter because she had no intention of wearing them for much longer.

She saw that the eyes of every one of the six men were on her as she reached behind her back to unclasp her bra. For a moment, she paused after she unclipped it. She gave them all a seductive smile before she let the bra fall to the ground. Her breasts were magnificent. Though they were almost always obscured beneath her habit, they were pretty large and quite firm. Her bras were DDs, and even so, her heavy breasts always seemed to spill out of their tops. Her nipples grew hard: not entirely from the cool air.

Monsignor Mark licked his lips unconsciously as he stared at her chest. "Very good," he muttered. "Very good. Now, for your next tasks, you will use those lovely assets to pleasure Father Jack."

She turned back toward the waiting priest. He had already shed his clothing, and his cock stood at attention, pointed directly at her. She certainly had never let a man fuck her tits before, but she had not been entirely clueless before she joined the convent, and she had seen the act performed once or twice in videos. She figured the first thing was to make sure his cock was nice and wet.

She dropped to her knees and scooted forward until his cock was level with her tits. Smiling up at him, she spits onto his shaft several times before working her saliva up and down. For good measure, she thrust her head forward and took as much of him into her mouth as she could. He was longer by at least two inches than either of the previous two but much skinnier. She could only get about half of it down her Tyler's throat, but she used her hand to work the saliva all the way down to the base.

—"Ready big boy?" she asked with a mischievous grin as she looked up at Father Jack. His face was blank as if in disbelief. He nodded slowly. Sister Kelly leaned her chest forward and took his long, throbbing shaft between her tits. The skin was warm against her chest, and she felt her pussy twinge as she pressed her breasts together, smothering his cock. It was nice a lubed up and slid quite easily between her firm flesh. She looked up at Father Jack as she fucked his raging manhood with her boobs. He looked to be in paradise.

His shaft was so long that she found she could easily take it into her mouth on the upstroke of each thrust. As the head split her cleavage and approached her chin, she lowered her head, opened her mouth

allowed it to enter. Now and again, she would stick out her tongue and swirl it around his aching glans. Each time she did, Father Jack would be forced to close his eyes for a moment as the pleasure rushed over him. The spasms of pleasure she gave him only turned her on more and more.

She watched his face as his pleasure built and built. The sensations of his throbbing cock fucking her breasts were heavenly, but she loved watching him even more, knowing that the look of pure bliss on his face was her doing. She had never felt so satisfied in her life. His face scrunched more and more, and she knew he was nearing a climax.

—"Come on, Father Jack," she encouraged him. "Cum for me. Cover my big nun titties with your seed. That's what you want, isn't it? Just do it already."

Her verbal help seemed to do the trick. Father Jack threw back his head and moaned. Rope after rope of cum fired into the air, arcing up before it splashed down onto her massive breasts. He didn't cum quite as much as Father Williams had, but by the time he was spent, her breast was amply covered in white goo.

—"Halfway there!" the Monsignor exclaimed. "And that means it is time for you to enjoy a little reward."

—"Reward?" She had not expected that, and as she looked at the next priest in line, she was not sure what was about to happen.

—"Father John, you are up."

Father John nodded and took a step toward Sister Kelly. He helped her to her feet and led her to the center of the room. This time it was the priest who sank to his knees. He looked up at Kelly, his eyes filled with lust. He grabbed her underwear and pulled it down her legs. She didn't even have a moment to register her own nakedness before he dove forward and began to ravage her with his mouth.

Her exploits with the previous three priests had already piqued her arousal. From the first powerful stroke of Father John's tongue, she felt as though she were ready to blow. Waves of pleasure assaulted her until she felt that she would drown in them. She could hardly catch her breath as the priest's talented tongue probed her folds with wild enthusiasm. She could hear the sounds of voracious eating as he sucked and licked her juices as though they were the most

delicious thing he had ever tasted. She wanted it to last forever, but she knew that she was much too aroused to last long at all.

When Father John added his fingers to the mix, she knew the end was near. His tongue switched to her clitoris as his finger plunged into her vagina. The simultaneous stimulation of her clit and g-spot had her cumming in a matter of seconds.

—"I'm cuummming!" She shouted loud enough for the whole world to hear. She felt herself release a stream of liquid onto the priest's face. Father John seemed hardly phased as he continued to lap her juices up like a man dying of thirst.

The orgasm shook her body for nearly a minute before it subsided. She stumbled backward, her knees like jelly, and she half-collapsed, half sat down on the floor. It took another minute or so before her breathing returned to normal, and she felt that her mind was once again working. During the orgasm, it was as though everything had gone blank as if she had completely forgotten where and who she was.

—"Excellent work, Father John."

—Sister Kelly could only nod her head in agreement as the Monsignor spoke.

—"Now, there remain only two: Father Thompson and myself. As the two most senior members of this group and long friends, Father Thompson and I have decided it best to enjoy your body at the same time. I believe the young people call it a pig roast."

The Monsignor gave a chuckled as he pulled the vestment over his head. Father Thompson did the same. Surprisingly, both men were already naked under their vestments, with raging hard-ons ready to go. She gulped as she saw their size. Both of them were massive, both longer and thicker than any that had come before. She felt herself getting wet all over again while her mouth filled with saliva.

—"So, who is going to be where?" she asked as she crawled toward the two fathers.

—"I will be behind. Father Thompson will take the front."

That was fine with Kelly. She was dying to be fucked, and she couldn't think of a better person to do it than the Monsignor. She crawled toward Father Thompson, only stopping when she was

close enough to open her mouth and have him plunge his cock into it. As Father Thompson pushed his fat, throbbing cock into her mouth. Monsignor Mark calmly took his position behind her. He gave her ass a hard slap, which sent a jolt of pleasure through her.

She felt him pressed the swollen head of his monstrous manhood against her opening. He rubbed himself back and forth, teasing her. She wiggled her hips in response, hoping he would take the hint. A moment later, he did. She moaned onto the massive cock, stuffing her mouth as another one pushed its way into her pussy.

The relentless fucking from two ends sent waves of pleasure through her whole body. She had loved each of the experiences she had had leading up to this one, but this undoubtedly took the cake; she had never felt quite this good. Two long and thick cocks were stuffing two of her holes simultaneously while four other men looked on.

Another orgasm was imminent from the double fucking. The sensation of being so relentlessly pounded by two men in two holes was sending her toward the edge. Her moaning grew louder as her pussy grew wetter. Father Thompson grunted in appreciation as her vibrations reverberated up his shaft. The Monsignor's pace

increased, and it seemed that all three of them were racing toward the same destination.

They went off one after the other. Father Thompson was the first. He threw his head back as he grabbed Sister Kelly's. He forced his cock as deep into her throat as was physically possible while he spewed a massive load of cum. The Monsignor was close behind. Even as Kelly struggled to swallow down her most recent gift, Monsignor Mark grabbed her hips and forced them back toward her. She felt the swollen head of his cock slam into her cervix. A moment later, she felt the warmth as the priest released into her.

The feeling of both men blowing their loads into her was the final push she needed. Her pussy clenched down tight against the massive cock that filled it, and she screamed into the shaft that filled her mouth. Her whole body shook as the orgasm rocked her for almost a minute.

When it was over, and she regained her composure, she saw that both priests had pulled out. She could still taste the seed in her mouth and feel the cum as it dripped from her pussy and then down her leg. The priests were all already dressed again. They had resumed their position in a semicircle around her.

"You have done well, Sister Kelly," the Monsignor said with a smile. "You have certainly earned you redemption. Even so, I hope, in the future, you will not be a stranger."

She smiled back. She certainly wouldn't be.

The Priest Immoral Game

—"I have sinned, Father, and I beg you to forgive me. It's been a week since I last confessed."

Mara's voice was calm, and she struggled to talk, but he could see through the square mesh that separated them that she was a lovely lady with long brown hair that obscured her face.

—"Child, tell me your confessions." He exclaimed, wanting to hear more of her dulcet tones.

—"I had sex with the husband of my best friend. I knew it was terrible, but I felt so isolated. I couldn't seem to hold myself back or stop myself. I'm really sorry, father, and I'm not sure if I should tell her or keep quiet. How should I proceed?"

—"The devil tempts us when we are at our most vulnerable. We can only make amends through repentance and prayer. Two Our Fathers and three Hail Mary's God bless you, child."

—"However, Father, you gave me exactly the same advice last week. Is my remorse the same as yours? I felt my confession from last week was for a lesser sin, and this one deserved a lot more..."

Mark had strolled into church a month before and been pleasantly surprised by how attractive the women who attended mass were. Young females with toned bodies hide their bodies beneath long skirts and lace gowns. He had imagined how they might appear if they wore less clothing or even none at all. He then realized what a fantastic idea it would be if he had a respectable position at the church. Something that drew people in and drew them to him. Only a week later, a priest at the Parish resigned, much to his surprise. Mark leaped at the opportunity, acting as though he'd been in the Parish for years and that this was his destiny. He was elected the new Confession Pastor for St. Constantine's church, and his duties were to begin immediately. He was trusted and respected.

—"In the eyes of the Lord, no sin is minor or major," he stated. As if he had any idea how the severity of misdeeds was assessed in the name of the Almighty.

—"Thank you, Father," she responded, believing his explanation totally. "I shall follow your instructions."

—"My kid, rest in peace. And don't forget to perform your confessions once a week."

It was the method by which he enticed most of the lovely ladies to return to him. His goal was to make them so reliant on him that he could infiltrate their lives more intimately. Jenny, Rita, and Beverly were the three women he had been close to so far. But there was one more person he wished for, Mara.

Jenny's house was cozy and intimate. Her living room was decorated in a beige motif with images of her family on the walls. Her antique collections were magnificent, and she had excellent taste in them. The shelves and tables that stood against her cleanly painted walls were adorned with all of Africa's history.

—"Father, please come in. This is where I call home."

—"Thank you, Jenny; it's pretty nice."

The ladies had agreed to have house calls after Mark persuaded them. Sessions where individuals might pray and chat about life's issues outside the church in a more relaxed environment. Jenny had

been the first to agree, and she was looking forward to welcoming him to her home.

He urged her to put the Bible away when she brought it out. They were supposed to discuss about actual life tonight, not necessarily Bible teachings. She told him about her past relationships and how lonely she had felt, how she battled with marriage after learning of all the adultery that had now entered the marriage institution. Mark agreed with most of what she stated, but he encouraged her to keep dating, follow her instincts, and trust that all will work out in the end.

Mark walked up behind her and embraced her as he stood against the kitchen counter, pouring them another glass of wine. He took the bottle she was holding in her hand and slowly placed it on the table. He then rubbed his hands against her breasts, her nipples rigid and firm against her silk top.

—"However, Father, are you permitted to..." She began to inquire.

—"Of course, I am," says the speaker. With a passionate kiss on the lips, he silenced the remainder of her words.

Mark spun her around and tore the buttons from her blouse. He also unbuttoned the skirt clinging to her hips and ass and let it all fall off her beautiful flesh. He sat her on the white kitchen counter, elevated her high, and then pulled down her cotton underwear without taking his gaze away from hers. She was drenched, and she was ready for him. He fucked her after unzipping his pants and pulling his stiff cock through the gap in his zipper. It was frantic, complicated, and exhilarating. She drew him closer to him by gripping the back of his pants. His dick was so hard, and he was so amazing. His need for her was so strong that he didn't have time to remove all his garments.

Rita and Beverly were both in the same boat. All of his house calls resulted in hot sex and intense passion. He fucked the ladies and fucked them hard. But it was Mara's moan that he was desperate to hear. He wanted her beautiful confessing voice to change into a severe, aggressive tone. He wanted to feel her fuck him like her life depended on it and see her fierce. He knew there was a pussy lurking beneath her long skirts and loose shirts, begging to be invaded.

—"I have sinned, Father, and I beg you to forgive me." My most recent confession was two weeks ago.

—"You did miss your session last week, Mara. My child, tell me your confessions."

Mara had not shown up as she usually did. It was as if she understood she was driving him insane. But now, on a calm Saturday evening, she was kneeling in the stall next to him. Even though her schedule was normally for Friday, he was glad she had come.

—"I had a dream," says the narrator. She started.

—"Go ahead. Mara, there's nothing wrong with dreaming. We don't have much control over them."

—"It was all a nightmare, Father. And I've been fantasizing about it for a long time."

—"What is the meaning of this dream, my child?" Mark was the one who inquired. I was curious as to what it was that was bothering her so much.

—"I keep having nightmares about you making love to me."

Mark fell silent for a moment, unsure whether or not to respond. He didn't know what to do, and he'd been waiting for her to say

anything like this for weeks. In reality, he hadn't expected her to say it first. He'd been preparing himself for the first moves.

—"Oh, Father! Please accept my apologies. I didn't mean to offend you or put your resolve to the test. I sincerely apologize, and this will never happen again."

—"Come to this side, Mara." Mark said, his voice steady and sure.

—"What? Father." Mara asked.

—"I said, come to this side." Mark repeated.

Mara arose, slowly opening the door and exiting her cubicle. She went on to the other side and opened the door to his. She found him there, seated on his chair with his black gown raised high, his hard dick in his hand. Not knowing what she would do, Mark said nothing and awaited her next move; it was then that Mara slowly raised her long skirt, revealing that she had no panties underneath, and slowly edged towards him, spreading her legs to sit on him. She let his dick enter him as she sat on it and let out a low sigh as he filled her from inside. She was so wet, and he was so hard. He had wanted her, and she had wanted him.

—"Have you been dreaming of me too, Father?" She asked.

—"Yes, Mara, I have to."

Mara began to ride him faster and harder. Each of them holding their long garments up. She bounded up and down, her breasts bouncing with her movements and her ass rippling with the effects. She occasionally looked down, watch as his dick disappeared inside her and how it showed up again when she rose. Mara bent down to kiss him, the both of them dissolving into a world of ecstasy and passion. Her moans echoed with the tininess of the wooden cubicle, and his groans seemed to roar. She fucked him harder and faster, her breathing becoming faster and faster. She let her long skirt fall onto her thighs as she decided to hold onto him in preparation for her climax, and he, too, pulled her tighter into an embrace. Within minutes Mara screamed with pleasure. Her insides are exploding. He held her tighter, motioning her into a way he, too, knew would make him come. Mark groaned as he came inside her in no time at all, unable to control himself and not to want to stop himself. After it all, he let his head rest on her shoulder as they both caught their breaths, then released his hold on her as she got up to dress.

—"Forgive me, Father, for now. I have greatly sinned." Mara said, and then she hurriedly ran out of the church.

Reminisce About Mara

Mara crossed Mark's mind often. There had been something unique and mysterious about her, and their encounter in the confession booth had left him yearning for more. She had sat on him, her legs wide and the lips of her pussy so wet. He had almost oozed with ecstasy when their bodies first touched, but he had held on, prolonging his pleasure and hers for as long as he could. She rode him and tightened her muscles around his hard dick, making him feel as if he was on a high. It had made him want to scream, causing a ripple of sound waves in the loudly echoing walls of the church. Instead, they had both climaxed as quietly as they humanly could, and she had scurried off without even turning to look at him. Mark waited each week to see if Mara would come for confession, but she never did. Instead, she had sent word that her mother was ill, and it was due to that that she needed to stay by her bedside, but both Mara and Mark knew what the true reason was.

Mark was barely able to know which sentence to start with.

—"I've been all right. Everything is all right, and mother is better now." She responded to each of his inquiries.

—"I apologize, Father, for missing so many sermons and confessions. I've just been going through a lot, that's all."

—"Let's go to my office and talk about it," Mark said.

—"Not today, Father. Maybe some other time. I really have to tend to my mother."

Mara ran off, and as he had suspected, she didn't return the next week nor the week after that. During the third week, Mara shyly walked into the quiet church and headed towards the confession booth.

—"Forgive me, Father, for I have sinned." She began as she always had done." It has been two months since my last confession."

—"Tell me your confessions, child."

—"I have let my family down. I was supposed to be there all the time. But I wasn't. I had too many things going on. I shouldn't have gone to class that day. I should have stayed home with her. I'm the

reason why… Why…. I'm the reason why she is dead. And that's why I'm paying for it."

Mara broke down into uncontrollable sobs. She sniffled and cried through each of her sentences, and one could tell that she was going through a very hurtful time.

—"Mara. Mara, calm down, dear child. First of all, it's no one's fault that your mother passed, God rest her soul. We are made from dust, and it is unto dust that we shall return. Think of it this way; she is at peace now. She is no longer in pain and doesn't feel any aching."

Mara's sobs got quieter as she listened to Mark's words and hung on to every one of them. She needed to hear this. She needed to know that it was not her fault. That there was nothing, she could have done.

—"It wasn't your fault Mara," Mark said as if reading her mind. "We cannot question the work of the Almighty, for he makes no errors. There was nothing you could have done that could have saved her."

—"But why am I suffering? Why have I been cursed if it isn't for this sin? Why Father, why?"

Mark couldn't understand what she was on about.

—"Explain what you mean Mara. I don't understand you at all."

—"Please tell me my prayers so I may repent for my sins."

—"One Our Father and The Creed."

Mara stood up and exited the booth. She seemed visibly disturbed and was in no state to explain what really was going on. However, Mark knew that if he wanted to see her again, this was his last chance to make it happen. There was a possibility that she would never come back, or even if she did, it wouldn't be anytime soon.

—"Mara!" he said, calling out to her while he ran towards her at the same time. "Wait."

When he caught up with her, he was panting and had to take a minute to allow his breathing to return to normal. He then lightly placed his hand on her shoulder, and looking deeply into her eyes; he searched for the words that would most likely, appeal to her soul.

—"I know you are going through a very hard time right now, and I know you must be feeling so alone with the weight of the world on

your shoulder, but I assure you, I am your friend, and I can be here for you. All you have to do is let me in."

—"I know a lot has happened between us recently," he continued, "but let's not make that stand in the way of truly helping each other when we are in need. I can just listen if you want me to. But the truth is, Mara, you need to speak to someone. You can't bottle it up inside."

Mara seemed genuinely touched by his words. He could tell from the way she loosened her stiff stance and allowed him to hold her tighter. Tears lingered in her eyes, and though her mouth opened to speak, she said nothing.

—"Come over to my place. It's safer and quieter there than it is here. You can come at six. I'll wait for you; whether or not you show up, I will wait for you."

Mara nodded, but Mark couldn't tell if the nod meant that she would come or a mere acknowledgment of the invitation. Either way, he had done his best and would wait and see. In his mind, he visualized Mara crying on his shoulders and him wiping the tears off her soft cheeks. He would then lift her chin and towards him and draw her closer into a sweet deep kiss. From there, everything else would just

become a whirlwind of passion and moaning. And the morning sun would find them through the curtain, cuddled in bed together, with wetness in between her legs and a stiff hard cock behind her.

Mara knocked on Mark's door at a quarter to eight. She had actually arrived earlier but had sat at a nearby park, contemplating if this was a good idea or not. Several times she had wanted to stand up and leave, go home and mourn the loss of her mother, but somehow, she just couldn't. After a long while, she just decided to go to him. Come what may.

He opened the door, pleasantly surprised to see her. When the clock had struck seven, he had convinced himself that she wasn't going to come. He had begun to contemplate calling Jenny and seeing if she would be free for the night.

—"Come in," he said.

Mara walked into Mark's cozy apartment. It was small but quite comfortable. She noticed that he must have had expensive taste as most of the countertops were covered with marble toppings. The kitchen that peaked at her from a slightly open door also had a grey

marble topping, and she smiled to herself. It wouldn't be wrong to live in such riches.

—"Can I take your coat?" He offered.

Mara allowed Mark to slide her cotton coat off her back, which revealed a loose-fitting blouse and a long skirt. She wore a musky perfume, and her hair was let down. Mara proceeded to sit on the couch furthest from his, and she crossed her legs, seemingly looking quite uncomfortable and on edge.

—"Thank you for coming, Mara," Mark said. "Can I get you anything to drink?"

—"Some juice, please, if you have any." Mara softly replied.

—"I have orange and peach. Any preference?"

—"Peach, please." She replied.

It was an hour before Mara had managed to relax and be comfortable in Mark's presence. She now sat freely on her chair and narrated to Mark how her mother had passed. For a while, she had managed to hold back the tears, but after some time, Mara just broke down into

uncontrollable sobs and allowed herself to be overwhelmed by emotion.

Reaching out for the napkins that were neatly but purposefully placed on the counter above the fireplace, Mark handed her one and moved slightly to sit by the edge of her couch.

—"Don't cry, Mara. It wasn't your fault. None of it was. Even if you had been there, she still would have passed. And I believe that would have been worse for you."

—"But at least she wouldn't have died alone," Mara said, continuing to sob.

—"Aw. It's all right. Come here. It's all going to be okay."

Mark pulled Mara gently into an embrace. He let her rest her head on his chest, and he rubbed her shoulder in comfort. Mara allowed herself to be held by him, to feel the softness of the fabric of his shirt against her face and to hear his heartbeat. He smelt of a minty aftershave. She wondered what he looked like naked.

They sat there in silence for what seemed like a very long time. Each lost in their own thoughts; it was surprising to know that they both

were thinking of the same thing; him inside her and her being made love to by him.

Mark knew this was his moment, and just as he had planned, he gently lifted her face to him. He let their intimate stare linger for a while, allowing each of them to be sure that what was about to happen was both consensual and precisely what each of them wanted.

Mara stared at him longingly, she had known this had a likelihood of happening, and honestly, she had somehow wanted it to. She had reminisced too about him and their encounter in the confession booth. It had been long before a man's hard dick had filled every inch of her the way his head. She had felt her pussy expand to accommodate him, and she had enjoyed every minute of it. Now here he was, and she had the chance to do it again, only better and for longer this time; she guessed it was this thought that had given her the strength to knock on his door.

Mark bent down and lightly and playfully brushed his lips against hers. He wanted to hear her moan. To hear her beg for his kisses. For his tongue inside her mouth, covering every inch of her. She puckered her lips, demanding more, but he didn't give it to her. Not

yet. Instead, he began to pace light pecks around her mouth and over her cheeks. He placed light kisses on each of her closed eyelids, then returned his lips to hers. He brushed them over hers once more, and she let out a low groan. She needs him, and his teasing was making her want him more.

Mark still didn't kiss her. He let his mouth linger over hers but decided to torture her with his touch. Mark slid his over her breast and cupped it. He heard her groan some more. He fumbled with the buttons of her blouse, and he slowly slid it off her. She wore a black lace bra, and her hardened nipples were now poking through it. She clasped the right one with his forefinger and thumb and rubbing it in circular motions; he aroused her as she had never been aroused before.

With her thighs wet and her hormones on an ultimate high, Mara gained the courage to undress him. She also removed the shirt he wore, revealing a well-built physique that glistened with light brown hairs. His chest felt so smooth when she ran her fingers against it, and she desperately wanted him on top of her. She wanted to feel his skin on hers, and she couldn't wait any longer.

—"I want you," she said. "You have proven beyond any doubt that I am yours whenever you want me and that I am yours for the taking, so don't make me suffer any longer. Please just kiss me and fuck me."

Mark plunged his tongue inside her mouth as a response to her sweet words. He had wanted her to want him, but this was more than he had imagined. Never had a woman spoken to him that way, and he felt as if he would explode inside her the moment he entered her.

Their lips and tongues danced, and she welcomed him with every inch of her being. He pulled off her skirt, without for one moment taking his lips from hers, and went on to unbuckle his trousers and pull out his now achingly hard dick.

Mara moaned and groaned, running her hands all over his chest and back. She couldn't get enough of him. She parted her legs and made way for him, and he honored her request but plunging himself inside her.

After his first thrust, Mara pulled her lips away from his and screamed his name. She needed to hear the intensity with which she had just felt him as he had entered her. She bit his shoulder slightly, all the whiling holding him tight.

Mara was warm and wet. Mark felt that his penis had just entered heaven and wouldn't want to part with it any time soon. He began to ride her, feeling the walls of her vagina rub and stroke every delicate and sensitive part of his long, large shaft. He was so aroused. She was better than he remembered.

They made love on the couch beside the fireplace for hours. It was the most fulfilling sexual experience they both had ever had. He felt her orgasm twice, and he climaxed just as much. But no matter how many times he reached his sexual high, he still wanted more of her and her of him. He just couldn't imagine himself pulling out of her and not having his dick in her wet pussy. She was so tight. So warm and everything about him sliding his dick inside her felt absolutely right. This couldn't be the last time that he would fuck Mara. It wouldn't be.

Mara began to shake; it was no surprise that she was climaxing again. Mark feeling her body underneath his, began to thrust harder and faster to assist her in reaching her high. He held her tight and allowed himself to glide over her body, pushing his dick deeper inside her when he went in and pulling it out slowly when he came out.

Mara continued to shiver, but she did not orgasm. This seemed unusual as the last two times; she'd climaxed pretty fast. He turned to look at her, only to see that her eyes were dilated, and it wasn't out of the pleasure that she was shaking. Something was wrong, and something was seriously wrong.

Play Sex

Many men and women play card games, cooking games, video games and perhaps even conservative games such as eye praise; however, not my bunch of buddies.

My buddies and I are distinct, and games night doesn't only mean getting rowdy about a game of cards, but it means a lot of fun. Most of us gather at one of the locations, and we perform a few raunchy sex matches. I understand that sounds a bit odd to a few of you, but it's exactly what we do, and trust me, once I say it's fucking hot, it's the highlight of the month.

We're a pretty large collection. Most of us have spouses; a combination of women and men who enjoy the very same sorts of matches. We get together once a month and pick the date that satisfies us best through our WhatsApp group. Most of us bring a jar of something, a few snacks and the celebration starts. That sounds pretty ordinary, right?

Well, allow me to tell you just what games we play.

All these would be the sex cards that we use.

I cannot recall who first purchased this sex card game, but boy is they utilized it to their full potential. The cards each have a different sex position, so we twist a jar, and the two people it lands on must conduct this position. You can jump once, but only once, or you're penalized by the group.

You can do this position entirely clothed or nude. You might also seduce the person you're paired with before getting into the position, as long as the entire group can observe. In addition, we have a rule where you need to remain in this position for 60 seconds for how long you desire.

We also utilize this trio of sex dice; we roll them in the center of the ring and take turns together by turning a jar. We like using all the sex cards to select what you utilize the dice with. The dice have boundless possibilities, and they'll let you know something intimate or something gloomy to perform to your preferred spouse. The dice let you know where, what and how to do these positions with your physique.

The first time we stopped sex games as a group was when we'd been drinking a lot. This was the weekend of the 4th of July, and we had

nowhere better to be than at the atmosphere of BnB on the shore. It was such an enjoyable weekend up to this stage. We'd spent the past couple of days in bikinis and swimming shorts, and couples were joyful while the singles among us were joyful.

One thing we all had in common that weekend was that we were all very horny. The beverage, combined with the relaxing setting, was driving us crazy in the bedroom, along with the couples among us who simply couldn't keep their hands off one another. Viewing that made the singles hornier and distressed.

I really don't remember who bought the package of cards and asked whether anybody was bold enough to play. Most of us sat in a circle and utilized a classic beer bottle to use as a spinner. It was just a joke in the beginning. Most of us understood how horny everybody was, and it became a small joke.

After the very first few spins, everybody still stayed dressed nicely in their bikinis and swimming shorts. The sex positions were played, and everybody cheered and laughed, but there was something in the atmosphere. Everyone needed it to go just a little bit further.

The jar spun again and again as we all viewed two of those singles in the group performing the sex position, but this time, she removed her bikini top, and his boner was totally observable. Nobody said anything; we were all just horny.

Their 60 minutes was up; however, they didn't stop and started exercising. We all kept watching. A person spun the jar, leaving them making out near the alluring fire. It landed on a few who went into the middle of our group. They peered around at us until she removed her buttocks, and he slid his thick, erect penis and slid it into her.

My mouth was open, and my very own pussy was dripping wet. Not one of us said anything because we all saw lust and jealousy. The couple started to giggle, breaking us from our trance. All of us understood then that today's sport needed a new significance; we had to measure to the mark and really execute the sex positions regardless of whom the jar selected. We all had to measure up the ring and do exactly what we wanted to perform. The excitement left my stomach flipping while I watched my buddies fuck. Being fucked with my friends was just like being inside of a few of my naughty fantasies.

Among my friend's boyfriends, the bottles spun to me, and that made me excited. He was stunning, and we make jokes about how sexy he was and how I must feel his penis inside me when he desired it. We met in the center of the circle and removed our tranquility. Our sex situation was the missionary position, and he set his cock to fill me up, which made me moan. His girlfriend cried as her nipples were pinched, and I could see a wet spot between my other buddy's legs.

He fucked me and my buddy. We were so blessed to have him each evening. After our 60 minutes were up, he didn't quit, and he kept on fucking me. His girlfriend leaned down on me and started making out with me.

Everybody was putting the jar down, spinning it, and picking up the card they needed to perform. Everyone really fucked, and everybody got to try out something different. There was no jealousy, so only pure, sensual fucking.

When all of us went home later this weekend, we pledged to do it once a month, come rain or shine. Most of us loved it a lot. We're still a standard friend group who only fuck and play sex games with dice and cards.

Daddy's Virgin

It is three in the morning. Daddy is probably fast asleep by now, which allows me to catch him off-guard. He is not getting away this time, not after what I am going to do to him.

Only wearing a bra and a panty, I sneak into his room. Lucky for me, he sleeps naked, making the process a lot easier. As softly as I possibly can, I crawl underneath the covers and head straight for his cock. Even though I cannot see it, I can feel how huge daddy is.

He shifts a little as I touch his relaxed cock. Scared that he will wake up, I jerk my hand back until he settles down again. If he noticed I was there, he was not saying anything about it. Once again, I enclose my fingers around him, and like a magic toy, it jumps to life in my hand.

It just keeps getting bigger to the point where my fingertips cannot touch my palm anymore. I think about how hard it will be to get it into my pussy, but at the same time, I cannot wait to make it happen.

I have been constantly wet and waiting for him to take me. The waiting stops now.

Without any idea of what I am doing, I kiss the tip of his cock a few times. Daddy shifts again but remains on his back. Then I wrapped my lips around the tip and started tickling it with my tongue. A slightly salty taste meets my tongue, and the throbbing cock begins to grow in my mouth.

I have seen how they do this in porn movies, although I am not sure if I am doing it right. Carefully I swallow more of daddy's dick, allowing my tongue to massage the curves as I go down. It is hot in my mouth, making me reach between my legs to play with myself.

After taking as much of daddy as possible, I begin to suck it while coming back up. Every time I repeat this motion, daddy gets bigger until his cock can stand on its own. But I make the mistake of letting it fall out of my mouth, which is when it slaps against his stomach and wakes him up. From underneath the covers, I can see the lamp on the nightstand being switched on. He lifts the covers to expose my hiding place, and with a shocked expression, he starts yelling.

—"Kate! What the fuck are you doing?"

He tries his best to hide his erection, but even his big hands cannot do it properly.

—"I'm taking what's mine, daddy."

—"Get out! Get out now!"

That's enough, I think to myself. I am not going to play nice anymore.

—"Are you seriously going to tell me you don't want this?" I sit up and cross my arms over my chest as if demanding an answer.

—"No, I don't." He retorts.

—"Oh, really?"

—"Didn't you hear me the first time?"

Without speaking, I climb off the bed. Instead of walking to the door, I head for the drawer with my panties inside. Daddy's eyes follow me, and before I can slide the drawer open, he yells again.

—"If you open that drawer, I swear I'm going to…" He warns me.

—"You're going to what? Spank me? If you didn't notice the first time, I liked it."

I continue to open the drawer and dig between the clothes.

—"I'm serious, Kate!"

It does not take me very long to yank out a pair of my white cotton undies, stained with both our juices.

—"Then what's this, daddy?"

With a blank expression, he stares at me, unable to say anything.

—"I know what you do with my panties, daddy."

I slowly walk back to the bed while holding up my underwear. As I reach the edge, I take the stained patch and place it in my mouth, then I start sucking on it, just like I did daddy's cock.

—"You taste so good."

Daddy does not know how to react. It seems like his instincts are telling him to keep denying the whole situation.

—"I don't know how it got there, Butterfly. And I don't know what you're talking about."

—"Okay, then I'll show you. Maybe it will refresh your memory."

I jump onto the bed and push his hands away from his erection. He tries to fight me off, but I am no pushover. Eventually, I wrestle his arms away and create the gap I need to prove my point.

—"You wrap my panties around your cock, like this."

He lets me stretch the underwear over his dick, which is still rock hard.

—"Then you jerk off like this."

I do my best to mimic his jerk-off session inside my panties.

—"Does it look familiar, daddy?" I ask while looking him dead in the eye

He does not give me an answer. Instead, he starts panting a little, enjoying the stimulation I am providing.

—"It feels better when I do it, doesn't it?"

—"Butterfly, please stop." He begs without any motivation.

—"I'll stop as soon as your sperm is dripping from my pussy."

Without warning, I bend forward and swallow his dick with the panties still around it. Daddy moans as his head falls back onto the pillow.

—"Oh, Jesus. Butterfly, you have to stop."

I ignore his pleading and continue to suck him off. His huge cock throbs against my tongue, and his stomach muscles crunch underneath my hand. He begins to thrust into my mouth, making me take more than I can handle. I gag a little, but daddy is obviously near the point of cumming, so I keep going.

Out of nowhere, he grabs my head and pulls me away. Aggressively he sits up, takes me by my arms, and throws me onto my back. He rips the underwear from my body as if they are weak pieces of string before he starts kissing me all over. Crazy with lust, daddy bites and sucks on my nipples and my tits. His hand is between my legs, stimulating my clit and probing the entrance between my moist pussy lips. I have officially released the frustration inside him.

Still sucking and licking his tongue, I ready myself for the moment he pulls back and penetrates again. Slowly daddy goes through the motion, and I can feel every curve of his cock as he does it. His strong pelvis grinds against my clit, transforming the pain into a pleasure I have never felt before. The pain is still unbearable, but the incredible sensation coming from our warm genitals motivates me to keep going.

Every time he pulls back and plunges forward, stretching my pussy beyond any level of comfort, I feel the distinct signs of an orgasm. But this is not just any orgasm. This is an orgasm with daddy's huge dick inside me, covered in my virgin blood and juices.

The thrusting becomes more intense. Daddy cannot control himself anymore, making him fuck me harder and faster. I can feel my blood and cream leaking onto the sheets as I begin to experience those first moments of a climax.

–"Harder, daddy. Fuck me harder!" I beg him while clinging to his body.

Without any reservations, daddy lodges his dick so deep in my pussy that it feels like it will stick into my throat. The panting

increases, we both start sweating, and our grinding genitals create a heat that could melt the snowcapped hills in wintertime.

—"That's it, daddy. Make your little princess cum."

Then it comes. My body goes into shock as daddy explodes inside me. He groans with pleasure while I find it hard to breathe, jolting underneath his weight. I cannot move. All I can do is let daddy spew his hot seed and drench my pink walls while I get lost in the nirvana. When I finally get my voice back, I scream like a little girl, motiving him to shove his cock deeper than before."

It expands and contracts inside my cunt with every load of white liquid bursting from his penis. My pussy is literally milking every drop daddy has to give, and I do not want it to stop. But eventually, it does. All that is left is my pounding heart and my hard nipples, pressing against his chest.

Satisfied and relieved, he buries his face in my neck, still breathing like a caged animal. And his cock remains lodged in my pussy, still throbbing with excitement.

—"From now on, I'm sleeping in your bed, daddy."

The End.

Sex Abuse

Good day to everyone; my name is Alla! I am now 28 years old. I want to tell you one story that happened to me when I was at the institute when I was 22. One evening, I stayed in the library after the lectures. It was already late in the evening, and my way ran along the road between the dormitory buildings.

But I will tell you a little about myself: at that time, I weighed a little more than 50 kg, average height, about 160 cm, long blond hair, chest size 3 of a round shape. In other words, an ordinary silly student dreaming of a guy on a white horse.

Therefore, when I was on the road, I had a feeling that someone was following me. Therefore, it turned out. A man jumped out from behind the bushes, grabbed my hair, and hit me hard in the face, which made me unconscious. I woke up in a forest chained to a tree, with a gag in my mouth from my own panties.

He stood aside and watched me. When he saw that I woke up, he said that not a single race was waiting for me and I should not relax.

He came up from behind and slowly began to drive his cock between my buttocks, slightly resting the head of his penis on my anus, which made my lower abdomen twist.

After he pressed and a member gently entered behind me, I shouted slightly. And the merry-go-round began. He pushes, and from pleasure, I have goosebumps. After about 5 minutes, he was finished. He wet the rag a little with some solution and presented it to my face, which I chopped off. I woke up in some basement without windows, my wrists were fastened to some kind of hook, and I noticed I am completely naked.

Behind me was my tormentor, who mocked slightly. Like I should behave myself, or he will act with me as a true rapist, if not.

After that, he took some heavy objects and pulled them towards me. What I exactly did not see, from which it became even worse. As it turned out later, it was a huge dildo on the engine (sex toy.)

It was arranged so that it was possible to sit on it, and another partner could fit on the bottom. In other words, he stuck this HUGE MEMBER IN THE BACK, and he settled down to fuck me. Oh yes, it was scary on the one hand, it is not known which hole in my ass

this bolt will leave, and on the other, I received indescribable sensations. After my rapist finished, he left, fixing me with cancer and sending a member to the vagina with the machine turned on. I do not remember how long it lasted, but I remember that after the fifth orgasm, I just chopped off.

In the morning, my rapist came as if nothing had happened and began to hammer my throat. I sucked selflessly, tried my best. To which he said that he was satisfied and wanted to fuck me from behind. Without any ceremony, he took the pulled chain, and I straightened up. He took a huge candle and stuck it in my anus. After tapping his cock on my buttocks, he entered the vagina and began to peck while he still managed to crush my boobs with both hands, toss and play with them.

This went on for about a week; no one noticed my absence, thinking that I had gone home. He then threw me somewhere on the highway and left.

Svetlana was going home in a bad mood. Her husband recently behaved strangely, and he avoided intimacy; she was annoyed. At first, Svetlana decided that her husband was in trouble at work, but her husband said that things were going well. Yesterday, Svetlana

decided on a serious conversation. She asked her husband to be frank. She was simply unsettled when she heard what he said.

The husband told Svetlana that he was tired of the monotonous classic sex. He wanted a new thrill, but he is not sure if Svetlana would agree to his proposal.

The proposal was as follows. Svetlana should temporarily submit to her husband in everything. Fulfill all his orders, desires, and whims. Even the most unusual. "Then," the husband said confidently, "our feelings will flare up with renewed vigor."

Svetlana loved her husband very much. She was ready to do everything so that harmony would come to their family life. She did not begin to question in detail what her obedience would be. She simply promised that she would do whatever her husband wanted.

In the morning, Svetlana woke up from a slap in the face. Clutching her reddened cheek, she jumped up and saw that her husband's face was displeased.

—"A lustful whore!" How dare you sleep when your lord woke up! On knees!

Svetlana already wanted to be outraged, but then she remembered the agreement so silently knelt. The husband sharply lowered her head to the floor and put his foot on her head. He suddenly turned from a tender spouse into an evil master.

"Remember, Bitch, and now you're my thing." Any disobedience will be punished. Otherwise, a divorce! Now, remember the rules. And he handed her a printout of the rules that a slave should follow. There were many rules, but Svetlana realized that she needed to obey orders without any question, and then everything would be all right.

Three months have passed. Svetlana mastered the rules in three months of training. Now her every step was connected with giving pleasure to her husband, whom she now called only "my Lord."

In the morning, she got up early, cooked breakfast, put herself in order, and then sat on her knees and began to wake up her Master with kisses. Only a member was allowed to kiss in the morning. The gentleman woke up. The member hardened. Then he just rudely fucked Svetlana in her mouth; she poured semen on her face and mouth. Washing sperm is not allowed. Svetlana went around the house, along the street, and shopping. After that, the owner went to

the bathroom. Svetlana sat down on the floor of the bathroom, taking on her body jets of Golden rain. The owner gradually wanted to teach her to drink his urine. He started with the body but then rose above the jet falls into the open mouth. Svetlana swallowed. She was already used to this procedure, thanks to which her sperm count became smaller.

Then the gentleman went to breakfast. During breakfast, Svetlana sat on the floor at the feet of the master, trying to guess his wishes. She either kissed his legs, or sucked a member, or licked his toes. Her master could throw her a piece from the table, which Svetlana would carefully take with her teeth, like a dog. Her bowl was in the corner. The owner liked to watch how, having unscrewed the priest, Svetlana varied from a bowl.

Every morning, her husband informed Svetlana what her name would be for the day. These were names such as "Nipple," "Creature," "Hole," "Bitch," and others.

This morning, before leaving for work, her husband announced to Svetlana that she would have a surprise in the evening. He ordered to set a festive dinner in the living room, put on jewelry, make bright makeup and hairstyle. Svetlana was delighted. She thought that her

husband was tired of using her as a slave, and today he will announce that everything will be back to normal. But she was disappointed that the table should be set for four people. And that she should meet her husband in her usual dress—a slave (naked, in a small lace apron), kneeling.

Everything was ready by the evening. Hearing the sound of the door opening, Svetlana knelt down, as usual, preparing to lick the shoes of her Master. The husband came in; three of his friends were with him. Svetlana knew two. They often talked; the third was her husband's business partner. Svetlana was dumbfounded. She carried out all the whims of her husband but believed that it was their secret. Her husband poked his shoe in her face. "The whore did not expect that today she has many masters! Now I'll bring her to life!" He said to his friends while laughing. He explained to Svetlana that all his friends would use her today, as he pleases. Svetlana had no choice but to obey. She licked the shoes of all four men and then led them to the table. Men could see all the intimate places of Sveta, so they made greasy jokes at her. While the men were having dinner, Svetlana was under the table, sucking all the members in turn. Men noticed that the slave had been brought up very well, but the husband warned that this is only the beginning. He told the guests

that Svetlana could be used as an ashtray, toilet, toilet paper, and most importantly—a machine for sexual entertainment. Svetlana served the three men all evening. At first, the three of them used her simultaneously, constantly changing places. Then the men wondered how many members each of Sveta's holes could accept at the same time. They managed to put two members in her mouth and fuck her. Having swallowed the next portion of sperm, Svetlana thanked her tormentors for the "pleasure" she allegedly received.

The husband did not take part in the orgy because he filmed everything on camera. He spat on Svetlana's face sometimes, calling her a lascivious bitch. He announced to his friends that now that Svetlana was prepared, he would like to make a film about a wedding. First, according to the scenario, a flock of dogs will run after Svetlana. The winner will become Sveta's groom. A wedding ceremony will be held, and after the ceremony—a mating season. Svetlana will be in a veil so as not to break traditions. Guests will be invited to the ceremony to watch the mating. In the meantime, the guests continued to have fun. They decided to play blind man's buffs. Blindfolded, Svetlana had to guess which of the guests fucked her in the mouth. After a few long hours, the men finally left the

Light alone. They expressed admiring reviews to her husband and agreed on a new meeting.

Svetlana was on her knees. She kissed all guests' feet and thanked them. Her whole body was in semen; all holes were filled with liquid.

After the guests left, her husband flogged Svetlana for "treason," he called her a prostitute for the night. "You understand that it's disgusting for me to sleep with you now," he told Sveta. All night Svetlana not only watched her husband's love games, but she also prepared their genitals for copulation-licked, sucked, and after the act—licked the anus and vagina of the prostitute. When the husband finished the prostitute's mouth, he spat out all the sperm in Svetlana's mouth, which Svetlana swallowed.

The End.

Sister and Brother

I had not seen Mark for a few weeks and wondered where he was and why he had not visited. I asked Peter, who told me he was busy with college work and preparing for exams, hence his absence.

On a whim, I decided that I would pay him a visit on campus. Mum had just finished baking some homemade apple pies, which I knew, were one of Mark's favorite foods, so I decided to pack some apple pie.

I knew the college he attended and the campus he was based at. I packed the pie in my backpack, wrapped in foil and a plastic container. I then got on the bus and headed straight for his campus, only about 20 miles away.

When I got there, I simply walked into each of the dorms and asked for his name at reception until I found the building he has resided.

I rang the buzzer to the number of his room, and a voice came through the intercom.

—"Who is it?"

—"It's me, Mark. It's Sandra," I replied.

Mark buzzed me in.

I go inside the building and go up to Mark's room that was on the second floor.

As I got to the door, it opened, and Mark let me in.

—"Hello Sandra," Mark said, with a surprised look. "This is a surprise. Is everything okay?"

—"No… there is nothing wrong," I said. "Don't worry, I was just so bored today with nothing to do and made a spontaneous decision to come and visit you."

—"I thought even if you weren't around, it wouldn't have been a wasted trip as I had always wanted to see this campus anyway and needed to get out of the house," I added.

Mark showed me in and offered me a seat.

—"Please take a seat," he said, pointing to the chair by his desk.

It was a small room with a bed, a computer desk and chair for studying, and a small TV set mounted on the wall next to the bed.

I sat on the chair, turning it around to face the bed on which Mark sat.

—"Would you like a beer?" He asked.

—"A beer would be nice, thanks," I replied.

He went out of the room and came back with two bottles of beer. He handed me one and sat back on the bed with the other.

I unzipped my backpack and brought out the plastic box with the pie.

—"Guess what I brought for you," I said, bringing out the plastic container.

Mark's eyes lit up with excitement when he saw I had brought some of his favorite homemade pie.

—"Wow, I've not had a decent pie for ages," he gushed. "Thank you so much for this."

Mark put a movie on and served the pie. I was not particularly hungry, so I let him have all of it and was happy with my beer. I watched him eat as we talked about different things that have happened since he last visited.

I watched Mark devour the pie and was pleased he really seemed to enjoy it. When he finished eating, he took the dishes away and put on a movie, and we continued our conversation with the movie playing in the background.

I decided to push my luck.

—"So, what do you think of me, mark?" I finally asked, not looking at him but down at my hands

I could feel the tension in the air. You could cut it with a knife.

—"In what way?" He asked after a slight pause, eyes narrowing as he sipped on his beer.

—"Do you think I'm attractive?" I asked, looking up at him. My heart was racing.

He paused for a moment as if trying to figure out where the question was leading.

—"Of course, you are. I think you are a very pretty girl," he said.

—"Do you find me attractive?" I asked.

—"Well, I already said you were…" he said, trailing off. "I mean, where are you going with this?"

—"No, I mean… do you personally find me sexually attractive?" I asked.

Long pause.

He was looking at me with wide eyes.

—"Okay, so where are we going with this?" He finally asked.

—"Nowhere," I said. "I was thinking, just curious. Because I had seen the way you've looked at me sometimes."

—"Well, I think you are very hot," he said, "And if you weren't my stepsister… well."

I could feel the electricity in the room getting charged.

I got up from my chair and sat on the edge of the bed, murmuring that the chair was beginning to get too uncomfortable.

—"Well, that's just a term, isn't it?" I said. "I mean, stepsister really doesn't mean anything. As far as I'm concerned you're just a black guy I know."

—"I know what you mean," Mark said.

—"Isn't it strange that we're supposed to be brother and sister, yet you are black and I'm white?" I said, chuckling.

We both laughed at this.

I moved closer, and I put my hand against his arm.

—"I like the contrast of my skin against yours," I said, looking into his brown eyes. "It really turns me on."

His eyes were wide now, and his eyeballs looked like they were about to pop out.

We were staring at each other. My heart was thrumming in my chest. I felt a hot quivering between my legs and thought the heat rushing through my torso would make me faint.

Suddenly we both moved forward, closing the gap between us, and our lips connected. His lips pressed against mine, and I instinctively

parted my lips and allowed his tongue to slip into my mouth. I could taste a hint of sweetness and beer from his tongue as a wave of pleasure swept through my body.

I moved my hands over his muscular body, frantically unbuttoning his shirt. He removed his shirt, and I rubbed my pale hands over his dark taunt torso and flat stomach.

He was cupping my breast, squeezing it, kneading it through my tank top. My nipples began to harden against the fabric. He slipped his hand under my tank top and began to massage my flesh, pinching my nipple and causing me to catch my breath.

After a while of feeling up to each other, he stopped and pushed me away. Then he got up to pull off his pants. His erect cock was huge, and the purple head was already glistening with pre-cum.

He got back on the bed and grabbed the back of my neck, pulling my head to his crotch area. I opened my mouth as his cock slipped into my mouth, with the head against my tongue. The salty taste of pre-cum sent me wild.

I rolled my tongue around the head and began to bob my head on it. His hand grasped the back of my skull, pushing me further and further down his hard shaft. I sucked him with everything I had until he began to moan with pleasure.

—"Ahhh, yes, suck that, baby," he panted.

After a while, he pushed my head from his cock and pulled me up. He kissed me again, slipping his tongue into my mouth, and our tongues probed each other wildly as we panted.

We were both kneeling on the bed now as I felt his hand move and caress the heat between my thighs. He clutched my mound through my shorts and squeezed, and I felt a jolt of blinding passion move through me, surging from between my legs up to my heart and down to make, my toes tingle.

He pushed me on my back on the bed and spread my legs. Then he pulled aside my shorts and panties and slipped his hand between my labia. His fingers probed into my wetness, dipping inside me and then sliding up to finger my clit. I shivered.

—"Hmm, it feels so wet and warm there. I want to taste it," Mark breathed.

He gripped the waistband of my shorts and panties as I lifted my ass off the bed to allow them to be removed. He pulled off my shorts and then panties. I felt his hands on my wetness as he parted my labia. Then his soft, wet tongue slid between my lips and raked across my clit. I gasped aloud as I lifted my hips to meet its touch.

—"You taste incredible," said Mark, as he began to devour me.

He slid a finger inside me and began to move it in and out of my pussy as his tongue licked my clit. I could feel my juices flowing down my ass. He removed his finger from inside me and sucked it, and then he slipped it back in and began to suck my clit with more vigor until I was writhing with pleasure.

Jolts of pleasure began to shoot through me as he continued to lick me. His masterful tongue stroked my gorged clit sending shivers racing through my body. My inner thighs quivered like jelly as I began to shudder. I cried out as I exploded in orgasm, jutting my hips up and grinding against his face. Wave after wave of pleasure moved through my body down to my toes until they were tingling, and it seemed to go on forever.

Finally, he got up and wiped his mouth. He grabbed his cock and stroked my glistening pussy lips with the head. He then pushed forward, parting my labia and entering my tunnel. I could feel my tight tunnel stretching out around him. He was so big, and I winced as I bit my knuckle. He pushed in deeper until I could feel him deep inside me.

He began to move in and out, with every stroke pushing in deeper. He drilled harder into me, and each thrust caused me to cry out in a mixture of pain and pleasure. My pussy got wetter as more juices flowed from inside me to lubricate the action.

Just when I thought I could not take anymore, he moved his hand to my swollen clit and started rubbing it in a circular motion, which drove me completely wild. A wave of orgasm blasted through me again as my legs began to shudder, and I had to grip the sheets very tight.

He was grunting and groaning as his thrusts got faster and jerkier. His cock began to pulse and twitch inside me as his hips began to shudder. I felt a hot stream of cum shoot out into the depths of my pussy, and it felt as if a hot stream was piercing my core.

He pulled out and warm wetness splatted on my stomach as he jerked off the rest of his creamy cum on my belly. I moved up to grasp his cock in my mouth to taste his cum and sucked him dry until he went limp.

We both collapsed on the bed, exhausted and giggling.

Eventually, he got up to hand me a towel to wipe the cum off my belly.

—"Well, that was fun. Thanks for bringing me a pie and extras," Mark said, with a wide grin on his face.

—"Can I bring you more apple pies in the future, sir?" I asked.

—"Of course," he said. "We just need to ensure our little pie-eating trysts are a secret… our own special secret." "Yes, sir!" I said.

The End.

Punishment by the Priest

Beth sighed as she examined herself in the mirror. She tried to persuade herself that she liked the way she looked, but she realized she was fighting a hopeless battle after what had transpired. Her curves had always been both a source of pride and insecurity for her. It was a two-edged sword, to be sure. She used to convince herself that men like women who weren't too skinny, but after last night, those statements seemed empty.

The only thing keeping her spirits up was the vivid memory of his expression as he ran out of the bar and saw her smashing his front windshield with a baseball bat. She knew she shouldn't have done it; taking retribution wasn't right, but it had tasted so good.

Of course, he deserved it, but she realized it didn't give her the right to do it. That wasn't the point of taking the high road. Nonetheless, it had been worthwhile in some manner. She was aware that she would have to go confession, but she felt compelled to do so anyhow. She hadn't gone in months, and though she wasn't very religious, she always felt better after unburdening herself.

She grimaced as she took one final look in the mirror before hurriedly changing into a plain sweater and blue jeans. It was late afternoon, which was her favored time for a confession. Most of the other priests had left by that time, leaving only one unoccupied priest wandering around. Even though all of the confessions were held in soundproof confessionals, she felt more at ease when no other people were there.

She was delighted to discover that her expectations had been realized when she arrived. The church was devoid of people. Her footsteps echoed throughout the enormous chamber as she looked for signs that one of the confessionals was being used by a priest, which was usually indicated by one door open (where the penitent would go) and one door closed (where the priest would go) (where the priest was). Each of the three confessionals' doors was slightly ajar. She smirked. Perhaps they had changed the time when confessions were heard in the few months she had been gone.

—"Can I assist you?" Inquired a friendly voice

She turned around, preparing to inquire about the confession times, but she came to a halt. A young and attractive priest stood in front of her, whom she had never seen before. She would have recalled

this one without a doubt. He was tall, with broad shoulders, and even in his sloppy cassock, it was clear that his torso was muscular. He had a powerful jaw with a thin layer of stubble covering it. But, despite everything else, it was the eyes that drew her in. They were a piercing green, friendly, strong, and passionate all at the same time. She could have stared into those eyes all day, and her mind began to wander to very unholy places as she did.

—"Um, yes," she responded, attempting to clear her mind of those thoughts. "I was on my way to confess." Father, have the hours been changed...?"

He said, "Roberts." "Father Roberts," says the narrator. They did, in fact, adjust the times about a month ago. "It's been shortened by an hour."

—"Oh, sorry for bothering you," she said, turning to walk away when she felt a hand on her arm.

The priest stated, "No apologies are required." "I'd be delighted to hear your confession. God is not aware of man's timetables. It is my responsibility to assist one of his flocks when they are in need."

She knew she should have just been grateful, but the sensation of his powerful grip on her arm gave her the chills. Those eyes had captured her attention once more. She attempted to remind herself that he is a priest while envisioning how he may 'serve' her. But, in the face of those eyes' depth and force, her better judgment was overshadowed by an unexpected longing.

—"Thank you, thank you."

He took her along a tiny corridor with a strong incense odor. And she trailed behind him, trying to relax her mind. She'd been ditched the night before—no, she corrected herself; she'd been duped. Although the rephrasing strung, she understood it was important. Before Stephanie arrived at her house, she received a text from Brad informing her of the news that Brad's 'breakup' was meant to foreclose.

—"Right in here."

Her thoughts of the past 12 hours were interrupted as she followed Father Roberts in a small room. The furnishings were spartan except for a massive bookcase that lined the back wall. Hundreds of volumes, some ancient and some new, filled the seven shelves that

stretched from one side of the room to the other. There was an empty desk to the left except for a lone yellow legal pad, on which rested a pen.

—"This is my study. I prefer a more personal approach to confession if that is okay with you. I find that hiding behind screens and walls only separates us and lessens one's ability to submit to the Lord truly. I apologize that there isn't somewhere for you to sit," he said as he led her over toward the desk and sat down. "I must admit, I am fond of the older style of penance, where one kneels before God to show humility for forgiveness. If you don't mind…"

He turned the chair to face her, and she kneeled somewhat cautiously. Though he had explained his reason for this room and this position, she couldn't help but feel uneasy. It was… unorthodox.

— "So, my child," he said, with his intense eyes staring down at her. "Tell me what brings you here after such a time."

—"Such a time?" she was caught off guard, wondering how he knew that.

—"You didn't know about the change in the schedule," he reminded her.

She felt foolish. After a moment, during which she could feel her face grow red, she answered him. "I haven't been here in a while, but last night things sort of went south."

—"South?" He asked in a calm voice

—"With my boyfriend... ex-boyfriend. Brad and I had been dating for almost a year, and then last night, out of the blue, he texted me saying that he thought we should break things off. I was upset but also shocked. As I said, it came out of nowhere. I was busying sobbing away, wondering what I had done, when I heard a car outside, and I saw my friend Stephanie get out and basically sprint to the front door. She was out of breath as I let her inside, and she had to pause more than once as she tried to get out the first sentence. It didn't take long, though, to figure out what had happened. She had been at a bar, and she had seen Brad… with another girl. Not just any other girl either: his ex-girlfriend Susan, whom we fought about all the time. She is a rail-thin blonde bimbo that Brad dated a few years before I met him. It always made me insecure… I'm not fat or anything, at least I don't think so, but I definitely have curves. I have a real body. That's what I tell myself. And that's what I believe, but I'm still insecure about it."

She stopped as she felt the tears welling in her eyes. She took several deep breaths as she tried to keep herself from having a breakdown.

—"I am so sorry to hear that he hurt you like that, but it doesn't sound to me like you sinned anywhere in that story." The compassion on his face was undoubtedly authentic.

"Well," she said, drying her eyes on the sleeve of her sweater. "I may have gone with Stephanie back to the restaurant, shouted at him, and then taken a baseball bat to the front windshield of his car."

She waited for the look of judgment from Father Roberts, but instead, he simply laughed.

—"Well," he said. "It is good that you want to make sure the Lord is not angry with you, but in this case, I think he has already forgiven you."

She was surprised to hear how casually he took the news of her destroying a car. She had expected to hear something about the need to turn the other cheek. But then again, nothing about this priest seemed traditional.

—"How old are you?" she asked as the question sprung to her mind. He was older than her, that much she could tell, but he must have still been relatively young to be so cavalier.

She quickly realized that it was perhaps not the most appropriate question. "Sorry. That was wrong of me to ask. Forget it."

Again, he laughed. "No need for an apology. I'm thirty-six. Somewhat younger than you expect a priest to be. And my methods seem unorthodox?"

He seemed to sense exactly what she was thinking. She nodded.

—"And now," he continued. "You are wondering whether I have anything to say about your story. Well, when I laughed, I certainly hope it didn't seem that I was not concerned by what you told me. I am quite concerned. But I think I am concerned in somewhat of a different way than you might expect."

The laughter and lightheartedness faded from his voice. The playful kindness in his eyes hardened as well. It wasn't anger or judgment, but there was certainly a strength there that made her heart beat faster.

—"I am concerned about how you referred to your insecurities."

—"You are?" she asked, not exactly expecting him to pick up on that out of everything that she had said.

—"Our bodies are given to us by God, and we should see them for the beautiful things that they are, especially for a woman as attractive as you."

She had begun to tune out at the first part of his statement. It was something she had heard before, but there was a difference between what people said and what they really felt. She had seen that with Brad. Those last few words, however, made her heart leap to her throat.

—"Me?" She asked.

He nodded. "Yes, you. I don't know much about Brad, of course, but I can tell you that cheating on a woman with a body like yours certainly shows that he doesn't have much going on between the ears." His tone was calm but stern. Confidence and power were lurking behind his words that made her begin to believe what he was saying. The intensity in his eyes, as much as in his words, was too

much for her. She was forced to look away as she felt herself blush—this time, it had nothing to do with embarrassment.

A body like yours. Those words echoed in her head. She certainly wanted to believe it, and it wasn't that she never thought it herself, just that so few people seemed to appreciate it. Perhaps Father Roberts was right. What was there not to like? She had proportions between her plump ass and massive tits that put skinny bimbos like Susan to shame.

With her heart still racing, she managed to lift her head to look at the priest again. This time his eyes didn't remain locked with her for long. They drifted down and stayed there. She felt a thrill go through her as she saw how entranced he was by looking at her body, by looking at her tits. A moment later, though, the realization hit her of just how strange this all was. He was a priest. This was supposed to be a confession. Much to her surprise, however, the thought didn't dampen her excitement. Instead, she only grew more aroused at the thought of how perfectly taboo this all was.

—"The problem is," Father Roberts continued, his eyes snapping back up to meet hers, "that this type of insecurity can fester and grow worse unless the right type of positive reinforcement is given. I

believe that as a priest, it is my solemn duty to help members of my flock in whatever way is possible... even if that requires unorthodox methods. Wouldn't you agree?"

She nodded her head yes, too nervous about speaking. Could he possibly be implying what he seemed to be: that *he* would be the one providing 'positive reinforcement'? And if so… what exactly did that mean?

—"Good," he said. "Well, the first step is to teach you to be more comfortable with your body."

Her mouth was dry. She could feel her whole body tremble in anticipation. Indeed, she was mistaken. Surely, he meant something else than what he was saying.

—"Why don't you being by removing your sweater?"

She thought her heart was going to explode when he said those words. There was no ambiguity now. She looked up into those deep green eyes, looking for some sign of a joke, but, of course, there was none. There was nothing except for an intense passion that made her lips quiver.

She nodded. "Of course, father."

Her hands trembled as she pulled the sweater up and over her head, exposing her bra to the lustful gaze of the priest. She felt a twinge go through her pussy. The priest did little to try to hide his stare. His eyes were glued onto her robust cleavage, and she delighted in the fact. To be wanted, as she could clearly tell he wanted her, did more to erase her memories of the previous night than anything else could have.

—"Now, the pants," the priest said, not bothering to lift his eyes from her breasts.

For this, she was forced to stand. Her hands were steadier this time, though they still shook slightly, more from excitement, however, than from nerves. As she kicked off her pants, she made to kneel again, but he froze her with a look.

—"Everything now." Two simple words, but the sound of them sent her lust into overdrive. She could feel herself growing wetter and wetter as her whole body filled with a fiery passion. First, she slid down her underwear, and then, with Father Robert's eyes glued to her tits, she reached behind and undid the clasp on her bra. As it fell

to the floor, she watched him watch her. The moment her naked tits came into view, she saw his face twitch as he drank insight. The look of pleasure built her confidence even further.

—"Kneel again," he said

She did, and now nearly eye level with his crotch, she noticed his massive bulge for the first time. She gasped at the size of it. It was hard to tell through his pants, but she was certain that it dwarfed the size of Brad's and probably of any other cock she had ever experienced. Her pussy ached now as she thought of what it would be like to be stretched out by something so massive.

Without a word, Father Roberts stood, and the size of his erection became even more evident. He looked down at her, his stare even more intense now that he was higher above her.

—"Brace yourself on the chair," he said

Not exactly sure what was happening, but more than willing to play along, she did as she was told. She stood up and then leaned over so that her hands rested in the air and her plump ass stuck out behind her. She turned her head and saw that Father Robert's attention had shifted to her backside.

"Well," he said, his voice dripping with lust. "Just as I suspected. Your body is magnificent. I've always liked a woman with curves, and yours put most other women to shame." He reached out and ran his hand along her back. She let out a small moan. When he lifted his fingers, she ached to feel them again. A moment later, he got her to wish, though not as she had expected.

She felt a slight sting as Father Robert's brought his hand down on her fleshy ass. She let out a soft moan. She always loved it when guys smacked her ass, and the thought of getting spanked by a priest made it even hotter.

—"Your body is beautiful," Father Roberts said as he brought his hand down again. "But you have not been able to recognize it. It is a sin to dislike the gifts that God gives us. And now you must do your penance."

Punishment by the Priest 2

He continued to smack her ass, and she was amazed at how much pleasure it brought her. The pinpricks of pain that came along with it seemed only to magnify the effect. Her ass bounced with each powerful smack that the priest delivered with his strong hand. The vibrations spread out across her body, moving her just enough that her pussy lips rubbed together and sent waves of pleasure through her body.

—"You have sinned," Father Roberts said as he brought his hand down once more. "Haven't you?"

—"Oh yes, Father!" she moaned as she felt herself moving closer and closer to an orgasm. "I have been a naughty girl, and now I need to be punished."

Each smack was more pleasurable than the one before it, and as she wondered whether or not she could actually orgasm just from this, Father Roberts suddenly stopped. Before she even had time to consider what had happened, she felt three fingers plunge into her

soaking pussy. The feeling that erupted through her body almost made her faint.

"Oh fuck, yes!" She suddenly wondered if the room was soundproof, but that concern vanished as the priest continued to fuck her hard with his three fingers. She could hear her wetness as he thrust himself in and out of her. The pleasure was building quickly, and she knew she wouldn't last much longer. When he added a fourth finger to the mix, she couldn't take it anymore. Her orgasm shook her whole body, and she struggled to keep herself upright as she braced against the chair, and Father Roberts continued his relentless finger fucking. When he finally withdrew his fingers, she dropped to her knees and rested her head on the chair as she sucked in great deep breaths in an attempt to gather herself. The whole world was spinning as she tried to come to terms with the fact that a priest had just brought her to orgasm during a confession.

—"Turn around." Father Robert's voice brought her back from her hazy post-orgasmic state. Though her body felt like she had just run a marathon, she managed to comply. She lifted her head off the chair and turned around, still on her knees, to face the priest. What she saw reawakened her lust in an instant.

While she had been recovering from her earth-shattering orgasm, Father Roberts had been busy undressing. Her eyes hardly knew what to focus on as she took in the glorious form of his naked body. His abs looked like they were carved out of stone as if they should belong to a fitness model rather than a priest. His chest and shoulders were likewise toned and muscled, and she could see the definition in his arms and legs. She loved a well-muscled man, and usually, her eyes would have been delighted to feast on his ripped body, but something else caught her attention: the massive cock protruding from between the priest's legs.

She had known it was large from the size of his bulge, but her imagination had not been able to do it justice. It was easily ten inches long and thicker around than her wrist. Her pussy throbbed as she thought of what it would feel like inside of her. Father Roberts shoving four fingers into her wetness had made her tight compared to the massive member between his legs; however, it was nothing. The head was swollen and purple, and it pulsed slightly with each of the priest's heartbeats. She crawled forward until it was only a few inches away from her face. With the most innocent expression she could muster, she looked up.

"Suck it," Father Robert's said, his voice deep and commanding. She had never been happier to follow an order in her entire life.

With reckless abandon, she leaned forward and impaled her throat with the throbbing cock. She gagged as she felt it slam against the back of her throat, but she only came up briefly for air before she continued to bob up and down. She could feel his shaft throbbing in her mouth. It was so wide that it stretched her lips almost as wide as they could go. Far from diminishing her enjoyment, the challenge of it only turned her one more. Sucking cock had always been one of my favorite things to do. Watching a man squirm and moan as she wrapped her lips around his aching prick gave her satisfaction like nothing else in the world. Feeling her mouth filled with cum was the ultimate reward for a job well done.

It took her a little while to get used to the incredible length and girth of the priest's cock, but once she had, she was able to force nearly seven inches of it in and out of her throat at breakneck speed. She shifted her eyes up as she swallowed an extra inch. She knew that guys loved to see her eyes water as she gagged herself on their cocks. Father Roberts was no different. He moaned loudly as she forced more of his cock down her throat, a quarter-inch at a time. With her

right hand, she couldn't help but gently circle her clit; she was sure her moaning only added to the priest's pleasure. Her left hand she used to massage the Father's swollen and heavy ball sack. She could tell just from how it felt in her hand that she was in for a massive load.

As Father Roberts' moans grew louder, Beth picked up her pace. She traded a little bit of depth for a great deal of speed and added in her hand to make up the difference. She bobbed up and down as fast as she could, using her hands to caress the parts of his shaft that remained exposed. It was clear from the sound of his moans and the speed of heavy panting breaths that he was getting ready to blow.

—"Oh, yes," he moaned as she continued to gobble up his prick. "That's good. Remember, you are paying your penance and learning to appreciate just how much pleasure your body can give others. After you have finished serving me, you will receive your reward."

As far as she was concerned, the big, warm load of cum that was about to fill her mouth was all the reward she needed, but she certainly wasn't going to complain about anything extra added to it. Her pussy was throbbing again, and as she moved her finger around her clit, she knew that another orgasm wasn't far off. But first, she

needed to finish off the jacked priest whose cock was currently plowing her face. Sensing that he was about to go off, she pulled his cock all the way out of her mouth, grabbed it with both hands, and stroked him as fast as she could.

With her mouth open, she looked up at him expectantly. "Give me your cum, father. I need it."

Those words must have been the last straw because, at that moment, he began to go off. Caught off guard by the force of his orgasm, the first jets splashed across her cheek and dripped down onto her naked breasts. She was able to reposition his spurting cock, and the rest of his load fired into her eagerly waiting mouth. She guzzled down his seed, delighting in how good it tasted. When he had finally finished, she leaned forward and licked the last glob of cum off the tip of his swollen head.

She leaned back and looked up at him, expecting to see him exhausted and satisfied. Instead, she saw that his stare was intense as ever and that the look of hunger had not diminished even slightly. His cock was still as hard as it had been, seemingly unaffected by the massive load he had just released into Beth's mouth.

—"Get on the chair," he said, his voice like a primal growl. "It's time for your reward."

She felt herself come alive with desire at the way he looked at her, the way he spoke to her. She had been with men before who had some dominant qualities, but usually, it felt a little put on. In the case of Father Roberts, there was no question that he was a true alpha male. He moved with a confident grace, his body rippling with muscles that Beth had a hard time pulling her gaze from.

As she sat down in the chair, she felt herself quivering in anticipation. Father Roberts took a step forward and then sank down to his knees. Her heart thumped. Her skin tingled. She could feel the excitement that built in her pussy and spread out across her body. He looked up at her for a brief moment, his eyes smoldering in a sultry stare. Then he shifted them down and dove face first between her legs.

His tongue brushed against her pussy, and she let out a moan of ecstasy. He didn't waste any time as his strokes came strong and fast, assaulting her clit with his undeniable skill. The sight of the muscular priest with his head buried between her legs was perhaps the hottest thing she had ever seen. His tongue moved with magical

precision, parting her folds and finding her most sensitive spots with ease, some of which she hadn't even been aware existed. The tip of his tongue teased him, trailed back and forth across her lips, before diving in and circling its way around her swollen clit.

She couldn't believe what was happening. This priest had his head buried between her legs and was going down on her so skillfully she almost couldn't get herself to breathe. It was as if her whole body was so focused on processing the immense pleasure brought by each stroke of his tongue that it couldn't deal with anything else. The feeling only grew more intense as Father Roberts wrapped his arms around her back and pulled himself deeper into her folds.

She threw her head back as her vision began to go blurry. The room was spinning, and she was certain that she would have fallen over if she wasn't sitting. Father Roberts continued the rhythmic strokes of her tongue as her whole body began to tremble. They both knew what was coming.

Too consumed by pleasure to even speak, Beth simply sank into the chair and let the feeling wash over her. The warmth spread and built, emanating from her pussy, which the youthful priest was busy licking. His enthusiasm was unmatched by any partner she had ever

had, only adding to the feeling. He wasn't doing this as a chore or simply as her 'reward'; she could tell he was enjoying it nearly as much as she was.

That thought was all it took to push her over the edge. Her body spasmed and shook as the most intense orgasm that she could ever remember ripped through her body. She let out a shrill moan that she was sure must have echoed through the entire church, but at that moment, she didn't care at all. She reveled in the bliss and ecstasy that washed over her, and when she finally was able to think straight again, she saw Father Roberts standing in front of her with his cock as hard as ever.

He stepped forward and, without seeming to expend any effort, he lifted her off the chair, spun her around, and placed her on her feet facing toward the chair. He leaned against her, and she could feel his muscled stomach and chest rub against her pack. She shuddered as his massive cock slipped between her legs and came to rest against her soaking wet pussy.

—"Bend over," he whispered in her ears as his hands clamped down on her hips

She did as she was told. As she bent forward, she cocked her hips up, and she nearly lost it as she felt the pulsing head find her opening. The world froze for a second as he paused. Only the tip had made its way inside of her, yet she could already feel how stretched out she was. And that was only the beginning.

With a grunt, Father Roberts thrust himself into her. The force of it was incredible, almost knocking the wind out of her. She could hardly believe the intense pleasure that filled her as he slammed himself into her again and again and again. The girth stretched her out in a way that she hadn't even realized was possible. Meanwhile, his length was too much for her to take in completely—even in her hyper-aroused state. That didn't stop the priest from trying, however, as he slammed himself into her as hard as he could, the head of cock ramming into her cervix with each thrust. She would never have imagined that that sensation would be pleasurable, but each time he crashed against her cervix, she felt like her whole body was on fire. It was partially the pleasure from being fucked by something that large, but it was also the idea of it that turned her on the fact that he was so large that her tight little pussy couldn't even take him all in. The entire situation turned her on as much by what was physically happening as by the idea of it. She was being fucked

from behind with reckless abandon by a priest of all people… and nothing had ever felt better.

—"Now, do you see how desirable your body is?" Father Roberts grunted as he slowed his pace, making each thrust powerful and purposeful. "This body was a gift from the Lord, and you should realize how beautiful it is. How beautiful this ass is." He gave her a hard smack as he thrust into her once more. "Beautiful these tits are." He leaned forward and reached around, grabbed a handful of both of her breasts, and squeezing them hard. "And, of course, this wonderful, wonderful pussy."

On the last word, he picked back up his pace and quickly accelerated to jackhammer speeds. Her pussy was on fire now as he stretched her out and pounded her at the same time, satisfying all of her possible needs and desires with his magnificent cock. Unbelievably, she felt a third orgasm building in her as Father Robert's breathing grew more and more labored, and the pace of his thrusting became frantic.

—"Oh yes," she moaned, finally giving in to the way that he was worshipping her body. "This body was a gift from God, Father Roberts. A gift for me, but also for you. Show me how much you

adore it. Show me how turned on I make you. Fucking fuck me. Fill me up!"

Her words put him over the edge, and as he began to cum, so did she. The feeling of his warm cum squirting into her pussy was too much for her. She felt her pussy quiver as it tightened around his member. She threw her head back and thrust back her hips as he fired the last few spurts of cum into her already full pussy.

She let out a soft moan as he pulled himself out to her. She could feel his seed running down her leg, but she was too tired even to reach down and scoop it up. Luckily, Father Roberts had a better idea. Once more, he turned her around with his strong hands. Her mouth opened in surprise, and he shoved his cock nearly into her mouth and down her throat. To her surprise, she realized that she hadn't had time to react or gag, and she could get almost the whole thing in. She took it in even deeper before she pulled it back out and thoroughly cleaned it with her tongue.

Now, his impressive cock was finally deflating, but even half-hard, it was larger than any other she had ever seen.

Conclusion

Thanks for reading till the end.

An Immoral tale is a short story that features immoral, often shocking, behavior—either as entertainment or to explore a moral dilemma. With the rise of the internet and social media groups, online readers have become more interested in this genre of storytelling—precisely because it's something that we can laugh at or gasp at without having to leave the house. This creates many controversies, with many saying that these stories are too shocking and violate rules on decency while others argue they're fascinating and enlivening. The debate will continue for some time, but one thing is sure: these stories can be immensely entertaining—even if they're only fictional.

Because of the myths we tell about sex, there are no boundaries when it comes to immorality. At some time in our lives, we've all been trained to be embarrassed about our sexuality. Many of us fall victim to the idea that having sex out of wedlock is something to be ashamed of—and that it is only acceptable if you're married. This

opinion is an example of a moral standard that many people still follow to this day—even though it's not the most effective one out there.

When you hear about immoral stories, you probably think of writers like Margaret Mitchell (Gone with the Wind) or Mark Twain (The Adventures of Tom Sawyer). Both these writers used their characters in immoral ways—from lying and murder to infidelity. However, what's interesting about these two examples they were simply writing stories that included provocative or shocking actions, which

In our culture today, many people still think that's why millions of people are still interested in immoral stories. Writing stirs something within us—an urge to experience the dangerous world writers create for their characters.

We can show people what are immoral stories by using them as an example. Perhaps what we need is a new moral standard that no longer focuses on sex. We need to start focusing on something we can all agree on to become a more interconnected society. What would be an acceptable action or a good idea? Should people get drunk, smoke pot, or die of cancer? Or should we focus on something else entirely—like encouraging people to help those in

need or even trying to include everyone in our society? Maybe the answer is not to have a moral standard at all but instead one that everyone can agree on, which doesn't restrict us from achieving our dreams and goals. Immoral stories can be a lot of fun to read—but they can also show people what immoral stories are.

Short Love Stories for Adults

Nice Relaxing Love Stories
to Improve Night with intense passions

Written by:

Skye Jenkins

Introduction

Love stories are very popular, and these are some of the best love time stories for adults.

Love stories have been told by nearly all cultures throughout history, as well as in many modern-day languages. With different love story genres such as romantic comedy, suspenseful thriller, sci-fi horror, and postmodern antiheroes being created every day and daily in the television industry, there is never a lack of good storytelling to fit any taste or mood. No matter what your preference is for genres or themes when it comes to movies or fiction books—these love time stories will make you smile (or even cry) from beginning to end.

The beauty of love stories lies in the experience when reading or watching one. This is what makes them so powerful! Even laugh at their antics, since you can relate to them through your own life experiences. These are some of the best love stories that have been written or created for movies, TV series, books, and other media forms. All of these are excellent examples of why reading or watching a love story is a very enjoyable experience.

One of the most popular forms of literature for love stories is books. Novels are a much more personal form of entertainment and can help people learn about different cultures and times throughout history. These can also be compared to plays since they incorporate drama as well as love and comedy into just one book. Some genres of novels that have been written over the years include science fiction, horror, romance, mystery, thriller, historical fiction, and many others. Love time stories are a popular choice for novelists who want to write shorter works with less complex plots and more emphasis on themes that are meaningful to their readers or viewers.

The television industry is known for creating shows based on popular novels or films. Many of these types of shows will incorporate love stories into their plots. These can be either based on a book or a movie. This is one way that writers and producers are able to add more depth to their storylines since the audience already knows what is happening, or at least some of the background information in regard to the characters.

For those who enjoy reading rather than watching movies or TV shows, reading love stories or short story collections can be a really enjoyable experience because they don't have any particular plot requirement. Instead, authors are free to tell stories with whatever

themes they want as long as they make sure it's interesting and captivating for the reader's attention span. These include science fiction, fantasy, romance, mystery, and many others.

Some of the best love time stories have been turned into movies and TV series by writers with talent. Love scenes can be quite humorous when they are well executed by actors and actresses in the roles of the characters on screen. No matter which medium you choose to view your love stories in, it is always a good idea to try to support whichever types of works you enjoy best. You never know that popular novel or television show you like may find a large audience in the future.

Been Thinking About You

All is fresh in my mind. I've been here for quite some time. There isn't anything that I don't see going on around me. Every move, every crack. Every single person who passes by. It's as if I personally know every leaf that falls and let it die. I will never leave, no matter how many changes. I recognize that the world has changed since I was a child. Even if I don't like the change, I continue to grow. I bloom year after year. When I take a step back to look at stuff, I sometimes don't realize how quickly time has passed. They alter, don't they? Others will notice that I'm getting older, but I've always been me. I'm the same freckly, blood-orange girl I've always been, but I'm aware that I'm special. It's strange to be in the back seat of someone else's car, so I didn't want to drive. I'm glad the driver was considerate of my privacy. Although it wasn't raining, I saw rain falling down the glass, which is soothing but also makes me feel existential. Why can't I be swept away by this storm? Toss it down the drain or into the river. Why can't I just vanish into the sky and

return with a fresh perspective? Oh, how I wish for such unattainable goals.

I seem to attract a lot of different things. I've been told I'm attractive. That, I believe, is why they rush to me. I'm tall but not particularly proud. I'm quiet because I enjoy listening. The majority of people need a good listener. That's why they approach me. They are well aware that I never pass judgment or make any statements. My recommendations are solely based on my personal experiences. In this fast-paced world, I implore them to slow down—at least for a while. I want to be the source of warmth they've never found in their own mothers. Since I am an orphan, I enjoy feeling like a mother. I was carried by the wind for a while before I found a suitable landing spot. After a lifetime of wandering, I suppose all I want is for them to feel at ease as if they have somewhere to call home. And I know I won't be able to track them when they leave. I dream that they take a piece of me, whether it be a flower or a leaf, wisdom, or something else.

Man, my life is a fuckin' joke. I've been squandering my time. And for what purpose? I'm here, peddling around town with nowhere to fuckin go because I'm a wuss. It's a guy. Is it true that I'm broken or that I'm not broken? Man, fuck those jerks. I'm not going to be a part

of that nonsense. I'd rather drive myself insane talking to myself than not speak to them again! Even if they call me, I swear, I'm not going to respond. No way. I'm not going to do it. I'm done thinking about it now. Just have to concentrate on me, and I need to unwind. What's more, guess what? I'm about to start walking down the street. That's right, I'm returning it!

I suppose no one has any morals any longer. I'm not sure why I'm so concerned about mine... But hey, I'm doing something right!... Right? Argh. If there are corners to turn, how will I know which way to go? I've been led down the wrong path. Now it's up to me to retrace my steps!

Every day, I miss him.

I know I smile now and then, but it will never be the same. They say I'm not old enough to be a widow, but I am! I've arrived. We all know that these things will happen, but there is no way to properly plan for them. Particularly when it's someone you know. We had been together for a long time, but it still felt like it was too soon. To get to know each other, I still imagine we're all seventeen and dancing. And while nostalgia can be a pleasurable experience, nothing about you now feels pleasurable. I'd like to think of you,

darling. However, it is excruciatingly painful. It's excruciatingly painful. It's the kind of pain I'll always experience. I'll tell them I'm fine and that I'm fine on my own. Maybe one day I'll be able to move on. Jimmy, but it hurts. I always assumed I'd take the lead because I knew the moment, we met that I couldn't live without you. I've always needed you. I'll never be able to stop loving you.

I'm just curious as to when it all took place. When we first met. In my mind's eye, I recall it vividly. I can't imagine how I'll feel if I have to return there. But I have to take action. You are far too unique to be forgotten. Maybe I'll get the same rush, butterflies in my stomach and doughy eyes. My spine tingles a bit. That is what I live for. I may never experience it again. I felt it even after fifty years with you. These are the times I miss the most.

When I hear another person approaching, her tempo quickens. I detect the scent of a young man struggling with betrayal. His heart is breaking, and I can sense it. He's barely paying attention as he pushes through the forest, tears in his eyes. I know those tears will fall if one stick hits him the wrong way. I want to cradle him in my arms as I used to when he was a child. I wish they didn't have to grow up to be men who compete for the title of most insensitive. I hope he never loses his sweetness.

"Hello. Andy here. Do you want one?" He extends a beer to her.

She is both surprised and pleased. "It's true. This is the ideal time to start. Thank you. My name is Amelia."

For a while, they sit and talk. I try not to listen to conversations. They'll speak to me when they want me to know what they're saying. For the time being, I'm just taking it all in. It's not often that love blossoms from the start. They have no idea that an old acquaintance of mine is approaching them. After her husband's death, she hasn't been the same. I wish I could support her in some way, but I know that just being here helps. She now seems to be hollow. It's as if she's a ghost.

"I hope you two are having a lovely afternoon," she says, deliberately startling them. It makes us laugh out loud.

The plucky girl blushed as she said, "oh, we don't know each other."

"Well, maybe you should, heh heh," the older woman suggests, and I agree. It left the youngster jittery. "Would you like a beer?" He extended his hand, holding an unopened craft beverage.

"Oh, yes, that would be fantastic. I think if I drank a beer, it would make my husband really happy." She seemed calm, thankful to have

her hands full and her eyes watching. Perhaps even a sympathetic ear.

“So, what are you doing here, like... What's up, ma'am?”

His query had taken her by surprise. She had not only not expected anyone, but she had also not known how she had come across.

“Ma'am? God, I’m getting old.” She leaned in close to me as she sipped her beer. It heightened the boy's anxiety.

“I didn't want to suggest anything, ma—miss.”

“Well, wouldn't you mind digging it a little deeper?” He was struck by the child.

The woman sat back with her beer and laughed, but it was clear that she was crying. She got to her feet and scanned me. I had a good idea of what she was looking for. I recall her in the same way she recalls me. I cherish every moment I spend with my children, but love will always be special to me.

When she found what she was looking for, she burst out laughing. “Do you see this?” She pointed to a heart cut into my chest, inscribed with her and his initials. “This was my husband and me.” People always ask if being carved affects me. But I’m curious about your

needles and ink, as well as other stuff on human skin. It's all fine with me, I claim, as long as there's something to it, “this was once a famous hangout spot. One time, one of our friends set us up. ‘Oh, jimmy, meet us down by the river!' said his friends. 'Meet us there, we're going to be with so and so,' his mates said, and mine said, 'meet us there, we're going to be with so and so.' We both turned up, but they didn't. They also felt they were really smart, ha!” Her smile was brightening. “We were a little irritated! It felt as though we'd been duped. But, guess what? She praised his handy work and said, "it was a wonderful date." Seeing this brings it back to me. She said, "I’ve never had a better time with someone I’ve ever met." She went on to describe their life together. Their marriage, their partnership, and their company are all in good hands. She spoke about the things she used to dream for and the things she now fears. It was the most she had felt since he had gone.

My citrus fruit teared up when I said, "I’m so sorry."

“Don't be like that, sweetie. Nobody is to blame. God wants what she wants and will give it to her when she wants it. There was silence. “If it was his moment, it was his time.” She finished her beer and said, "though I sometimes wish it was also mine." “It's probably best if I get started.”

"Do you mind if we hug... Miss?" Andy had been moved by her tales. Amelia found it endearing to see such a soft side of this boy she had only just met.

"That would be fantastic, honey!" Thank you." They all hugged for a few moments. It was unavoidable to cry. But being there together in this way was a joyous occasion. She left that day, and I'm not sure if she'll return.

"Perhaps we should carve our names as well. With a shy smirk, she suggested, "just in case." He looked at her as if they'd known each other for a long time. I'm familiar with the appearance of passion. He took out a knife and started cutting. "you'll have to spell it out for me."

And I recall those days vividly, each one as brilliant as the last. At the moment, they seem insignificant, but they add up to be life-changing events in our lives. And the love we have for one another is the same love we have for plants, trees, and everything else.

All About Books and Bread

I exhaled a sigh of relief as the last guest exited the library gate. Anything that might have gone wrong today did, and I was happy to take off my shoes and finish a few things before going home for the evening.

The cart's rusty, tired wheels squeaked softly as I moved it down the aisles, pausing only when I needed to return a book to its alphabetical shelf position. This aspect of my work has always been one of my favorites. The serenity and quiet of an empty library are indescribable. I'm alone with my thoughts and the wonderful scent of books.

When I heard a noise, I turned the corner to the next aisle. As I listened intently, my feet came to a halt. From somewhere inside the house, I could hear faint music being played. As I tried to figure out where the music was coming from, I slowly turned in a circle. "How are you?" I yelled something. "The library is now closed."

There was no answer. I walked away from the book cart and toward the source of the light and music.

“How are you?” My voice was slightly shaky from nerves as I asked again.

As I got closer, I detected the distinct sounds of 90s R&B and detected a delectable aroma. I wasn't sure what it was, but it smelled like garlic and tomato sauce to me. My mouth started to dry up. “What the hell is going on?” I wondered.

I slowly crossed the aisle and immediately came to a halt because I couldn't believe what I was seeing.

“Alex!” exclaims the speaker.

He casually responded, "Hi, babe."

“What are you doing here?”

“I decided to catch you off guard. With a sly smile on his mouth, he said, "Surprise."

My eyes gleamed. “You did it!” “How did you get in here?” “Remember a few weeks ago when you were struggling with those rowdy adolescents in the computer lab? As I rushed in with all of

this, they kept you pleasant and occupied," his right hand gestured to the rest of the surprise he had set up.

A traditional red and white checkered picnic blanket, a bottle of red wine with glasses, and two plates filled with delicious-smelling food were placed on the floor between the two rows of books.

"Alex," I exclaimed, stunned. "Wow, this is amazing! I'm not sure how you did it."

"I knew your day wasn't going well because of all the texts you sent me during your shift. I just wanted to bring a smile to your face." I couldn't believe what I was hearing. Tears welled up in my eyes. "Aww, Sophie, what's the matter?" he inquired.

I approached him and wrapped my arms around him. His arms encircled my waist and drew me in closer. "Thank you," I whispered in his ear as I fought back tears.

"You're welcome, my love," he squeezed me a little tighter.

We stood there for a few moments, holding each other when my stomach let out a very loud, very noticeable growl. We both burst out laughing. "I think I'm starving."

"I suppose so," Alex said. We both took a small step back as our embrace came to an end.

"It's understandable. I didn't even take a break to eat today because I was too busy putting out fires and doing my regular tasks."

"All right, let's get that straightened out. "Baby, take a seat."

He gently kissed my lips before bending down to pour the wine. I took a seat in front of one of the dishes, a napkin on my lap. "Honey, these smells and looks great. Is this something from Gino's?"

"Of course!" says the speaker. It's eggplant parmesan, your preference. I also requested additional bread, oil, and vinegar. Let me check to see if it was put in here."

I couldn't help but smile as I watched him rummage through the take-out packages. I felt a strong sense of gratitude and affection wash over me. He knew I'd had a rough day and went out of his way to pick up my favorite meal and surprise me with this date. He didn't have to because I didn't ask him to. It wasn't enough for me to do so. He recognized that I needed something to brighten my day and went out of his way to provide it. That's the type of person he is. Thoughtful, caring, and loving are three words that come to mind when I think of you. I must be the luckiest woman on the planet.

He exclaimed, "A-ha!" "Here it is!" exclaims the. With a beaming smile on his beautiful face, he took a plastic container from the bag and turned to me. He slid it open and handed it to me. "Help yourself, baby."

I reached for a slice of crusty Italian bread and said, "Thank you." It was still wet, and the scent was heavenly. "Bread is one of my favorite foods."

"I know you do, baby," Alex chuckled. He took the oil and vinegar from the bag and reached back into it. "Let me spill these out on a plate for us to dip in."

He put the plate in front of us, next to the bread. Our gazes collided. I expressed my gratitude by saying, "Thank you for doing this."

"You're welcome, lovely." He kissed me on the lips as he bent over. "Now eat your dinner before it gets cold. I know you're hungry."

I grinned and got to work. I moaned with pleasure as soon as the food was put on my lips. "Oh, my God. This is just delicious."

"I'm glad you're having a good time, baby."

"I'm overjoyed. "Mmmm," I exclaimed as I did a happy dance.

As he watched me, he said, "My baby loves her food." "You're the cutest thing I've ever seen."

I took another forkful of food and said, "Thank you, honey." "Have you had a good day?"

"It was a fairly uneventful day. Meetings are a must. Reports are what they're called. "It's the same old stuff."

"Wow, that's fantastic. I'm relieved to learn that there were no big problems. You've been very busy down there recently."

"Yeah, but it seems that things are winding down. Fortunately."

For a few minutes, we sat in silence, eating and sharing glances. The music was still playing softly in the background, its slow, melodic sounds calming my nerves. One of my favorite songs' familiar beat filled the space. I began to sway and gently sing along. Alex rose to his feet and extended his hand towards me.

"Baby, come here."

I gave him a friendly smile and took his hand in mine. He assisted me in standing up and then led me to an open area not far from where we had been dining. He took my hand in his and encircled my waist with his other arm. We shifted to the rhythm of the song; our

bodies fused together. His hands pushed against the small of my back, drawing me closer to him. I sighed, feeling completely at ease in my husband's embrace. What started out as a frustrating, hectic day turned out to be a wonderful surprise. The pressures that had been plaguing me had vanished, leaving only love in their wake.

The Wrong Relationship

I checked my phone repeatedly, but there was no call. Even though it is 1 p.m., there has been no call or message from her. She generally texts me first thing in the morning. A thought keeps running through my mind: why hasn't she messaged me yet?

As I was thinking about her, I had a flashback to how it all began. How she came into my life, how I tried to restrict her involvement but was unable to do so. She was becoming more and more valuable to me with each passing day. She is one of the most precious things in my life that I have managed to keep hidden from others. She is my hidden lover, and I am her hidden admirer. She makes me happy, and when she leaves, my heart sinks, and I look forward to hearing from her every day.

I checked my phone once more, but there was no call. My heart began to sink. On weekdays, we chat while working in our offices. Monday through Friday. 9 to 7 means a lot to both of us because it gives us time to talk and get to know each other better. The time had passed, and it was now 3: 30 p.m., but there had been no

communication from her. I was telling myself that she was probably busy or trapped somewhere, which is why she didn't contact me. It was difficult for me to let go of the day. It's Friday, and we don't talk on weekends, so I'm not sure how I'll feel if I don't talk to her for more than three days.

I didn't want this weekend to come. It was agonizing for me to have to wait until Monday to hear from her. On Monday, I waited for her message once more. Hours passed with no message from her; I considered calling her but realized I couldn't. I was in a bind and felt powerless. I only wanted to hear from her once and find out what was up. Why isn't she speaking to me?

A week has passed in this manner. There was no physical touch. I was feeling down. I wanted to call her today just to find out where she was. However, I waited. I then texted her.

Hello!

I was hoping for a blue tick. And, yes, she read it, and I can see her typing. My face lit up, and I waited for her answer with bated breath.

Hello there!

It came from the other side.

Did I start asking her questions? I questioned her about her whereabouts, and she responded. "I'm great. I was working in the workplace. On Thursday, I had an emergency trip to Kashmir, where my personal phone number had gone out of service. I was so preoccupied that I couldn't take a break. I apologize."

I felt at ease, but I was also aware of how precious she had become to me. Initially, I refused to let her into my life, but now I refuse to let her go. I'd never felt the strength of our bond before. I've grown fond of her by this point.

And then it hit me: we're both married, with our own set of commitments to our families and jobs. This is exactly what she was doing. I was wondering if I was on the right track.

I Promised

"I'm sorry to say this, Duncan. You would almost definitely not be able to lift your legs as a result of mild sedation during the operation. However, I guarantee that daily physiotherapy will alleviate it. I promise... Be brave and don't lose faith."

I attempted to get up again. Oh, my God! I'm unable to lift my legs. My sorrow poured out in a torrent of uncontrollable tears as I collapsed on the bed in a disheveled heap.

I was diagnosed with third-stage cancer a year and a half ago. I was devastated at the time.

"Doctor... Is this disease curable? I need a clear image of it."

"Doctor... Please don't keep something from me."

"Um... Duncan, please calm down. Our expert team is here to support you. What we need is your unwavering support. We pledge to do everything in our power to ensure your survival.

From that day forward, I tried to work with them. I had my first surgery a week ago, hoping that my doctors would follow through with their word. Every time, they assure me that everything is going to be fine. Duncan's life will be altered as a result of this surgery. This time, I didn't need them to give me any more hope.

They did, however, come up with new hope and pledge.

I couldn't take the pain any longer. My chest was ripped open by gut-wrenching sobs. Like a serpent, grief, pain, and suffering encircled me. Every promise made to me was a waste of time. Promises, like pie crust, are made to be broken...

This way of life drains me. "Oh, no!" Please, God, take my life..."

"Duncan... Did you know there are a total of eighteen stairs to climb to get to my house? I'm not going to get you up. You must climb it on your own."

I took out my phone and read the message several times. It came from Adele the love of my life.

When I read it for the first time, I exploded like a volcano. I was frantic because of my condition, and he's feigning something.

My rage dwindled with each reading. "What did he really mean?"

Consider the probability that I died during the procedure. It did not happen. I regained my life. But there was always hope.

"I'd like to go for a walk..."

"I want to live normally, free of the stench of drugs and the agony of chemo."

"What else... I'd like to climb some number of stairs."

"If you don't get what you want, change your mindset."

He taught me the most important lesson.

That is why I admire him. Not only because of the deep love he showers on me. He brought light into my life. Never sympathizes with my situation. I didn't feel the need to justify something. Through my single breath, he understands. Happiness is a mindset, they taught me. The amount of work is the same whether we make ourselves unhappy or happy.

When I proposed to him, the only thing he wanted was for me to never leave him, no matter what...

"Adele... I promise you that I am going to do everything in my power to live and remain with you forever..."

I responded via text...

I promised.

"No matter how debilitating our difficulties, disappointments, and difficulties are, they are only temporary. Whatever happens to you, whatever death does to you or your loved ones, the resurrection will always promise you a future..."

"The resurrection gives us a new and perfect existence in the future, God loves you too much to abandon us to deal with the suffering, remorse, and loneliness of this life..."

I can understand that better now that I am sitting beside him in his house.

When Duncan tied the nuptial knot around my waist, I vowed to cherish him every day for the rest of my life...

I laid down my diary.

"Adele... get up."

When he stood up, I handed him a card that read...

"I promise you that I will keep every promise I have made to you up to this point..."

"Happy Anniversary, Baby..."

Happy Addiction

"Sometimes you act strangely," Andrea said, her gaze fixed on Richard like an arrow. Andrea's words frightened Richard, who was totally unaware of his own presence. He swallowed his saliva, cleared his throat, and took her left hand in his.

"Our journey has been so rhythmical from the moment I first saw you until now; we loved each other unconditionally, waited for hours in different places just to catch a glimpse of each other, and our ears tried hard to find and listen to each other's voice."

"But you know what happens when you're too available? It's true that too much familiarity breeds contempt. We became familiar, close, and blunt. We broke all the boxes and crossed all the boundaries. Now, tell me honestly, why did you perceive me as a stranger? It's because we've crossed all the boundaries, and there are no more interesting and attractive things between us."

"That isn't what I mean to say," Andrea said after a deep breath.

Richard loosened Andrea's grip and took a stern tone. People were leaving the park where Andrea and Richard met every late afternoon. It was evening.

Andrea was standing when Richard offered her his seat on a local bus, and it was their first encounter. Later, it was discovered that they were both applying to the same university for admission.

They were accepted, and after a few days of ruminating, they exchanged phone numbers. They rode the same bus every day, and after just a few weeks, they were so close that taking separate classes seemed like a punishment for both of them.

Their first physical contact occurred while walking on a muddy road on a rainy day. When Andrea stumbled, Richard almost inadvertently took her hand and squeezed it so tightly that Andrea couldn't move an inch. There were no emotions at the time because everything happened in the blink of an eye, but this accident later became one of their fondest memories.

They were happy friends, just friends, and nice friends, and all was going swimmingly before the poetry affected both of them, and they began to grow feelings for one another. They began spying on each other now. Andrea couldn't stand Richard talking to other people,

and Richard became so protective of Andrea that he couldn't stand her going through a location where boys could notice her. They were on the verge of being envious. But all of this happened so quietly that neither Richard nor Andrea was alarmed. They had no idea what was going on with both of them.

With each passing day, their feelings grew stronger, and they became almost addicted to each other. And, as the saying goes, "addiction is more dangerous than love." For them, this was becoming real. Both of them felt compelled to express their feelings to each other at this stage. They were about to make a huge blunder. And what they felt for each other was more of an addiction and a fleeting bond than love. However, they were unaware of this and shared almost all that was on their minds.

The idea of sharing their feelings seemed cool to them, and they felt relieved because they both felt the same way and understood each other's concerns. But what happened next was that they had crossed some lines and were now blaming each other for small and insignificant mistakes that they didn't consider mistakes when they were just friends. It meant they were now tethered to a natural power. Their living habits shifted as a result of what was going on between them, and they were no longer who they were.

They began blaming each other for minor misfortunes and hurling insults at each other that were more caustic than anything else. "So, you think you're cool and clever, huh!" Richard once said to Andrea. “But no, you aren't; in fact, you're a narcissist."

And their relationship was already spiraling out of control. They couldn't do anything because it wasn't based on love and empathy, but rather on needs, envy, temporary addiction, and manipulations.

To keep the situation under control, Andrea said, "That isn't what I mean to say," but she knew deep down that this matter needed to be resolved today, right now, so she also threw her card by saying, "That isn't what I mean to say."

"Don't you think we were more at ease when we were just friends, Richard?"

"Of course, we were more relaxed and happier when we were just friends," Richard said, instinctively realizing the nuances concealed in Andrea's words. "Yes, I really miss our friendship more than anything else."

Andrea heard what he was doing and agreed with him. "What if we were those 'only mates' again? wouldn't that be gratifying?" she asked amusingly.

And there it was, the thing they'd all been wanting to say, the words they'd been waiting to say. They missed their friendship and were fed up with the shackles they were forced to wear as a result of their meticulous relationship.

For the first time in two months, they were both happy because they finally realized what they really wanted. They were so enamored with each other that they forgot to loosen each other's grip.

They boarded the same bus the next morning, sitting next to each other, gossiping about things they both knew about and staring at each other for a brief moment, completely unaware of what had happened the night before. They may have forgotten something, or they just did not want to recall what happened that night.

They got off the bus at the university gate and began walking quietly and respectfully alongside one another. They were at the entrances of their respective departments in less than five minutes, and they both said their goodbyes in their eyes without saying a word. They didn't return their stares and went into their respective offices.

Perhaps they were friends at this stage. Perhaps friendship is a partnership as well.

Renewed

Audrey closed her eyes and looked out over the Caribbean Sea, a light breeze brushing against her skin, the white sand warm between her bare toes. The place was breathtakingly beautiful, but it couldn't take away her sadness as she recalled the last time she'd been here.

But it seems like such a long time ago. In only a few years, a lot can change—a lot of heartbreak can change a person and push a wedge through all the strongest bonds, breaking even the deepest love. They returned three years later, this time for one of the island's equally infamous quickie divorces rather than the beachside marriages for which it was famous.

Audrey sighed deeply, her sigh tinged with pain and sorrow. How could this lovely spot, with its lush green coastline, endless azure blue sea, and endless sands, be a place for the pain she was experiencing right now?

The guy stood at the edge of the palm trees, waiting. He couldn't pull his eyes away from the dark-haired woman standing at the water's edge, looking out to sea as if she was expecting something—or

something. Her slender figure, dressed in a loose flowing cotton dress, her wild hair, and bright blue eyes not dissimilar to the color of the sea, made her stunning. But it wasn't her beauty that drew him in; in his job as a freelance photographer, he met a lot of beautiful people. He was drawn to her by her isolation and intensity. Even from a distance, he could tell she was unlike any other woman he'd ever met.

Even before she turned around, Audrey heard the man approaching. She was conscious that he was looking at her and had a peculiar sense of calm about being watched. When she looked at him, she felt an immediate bond that she had only felt once before. He approached her slowly, and they exchanged glances. It felt like I was meeting an old friend on a mysterious beach, not a stranger.

Later, as they sat in one of the resort's several pubs, sipping local drinks, they started to converse. The first impressions, their hotels, the food quality, and the friendliness of the locals. Their talk was oddly tentative, given their earlier meeting's naturalness and confidence. By mirroring each other's gestures and speaking directly into each other's eyes, onlookers may have picked up on the overt flirtation. The discussion only deepened later, after the alcohol had had its loosening effect. They talked about why they were here, and

Audrey eventually opened up about her heartache from last year and how events had brought her back to the place where she had married the only man, she thought she could ever love. She told him the stuff she couldn't tell anyone about because they were hidden deep inside her. She told him about how she felt after losing her daughter.

When the pains began, she was six months pregnant and the happiest she had ever been. Since Burley was working out of town, she was living with her mother. He hadn't returned in time. It was just one of those things, the doctor said, and they should try again. But how could she when she couldn't even meet Burley's gaze? She despised him at the time for not being there, for not suffering as badly as she did, and most of all for resembling the tiny baby boy she had owned for just three hours before he was taken away. She withdrew from her husband, relatives, and friends over the next few months. It would have been a betrayal to her son if she had refused to recover from the pain she was experiencing. She had declined to stand next to her husband at the funeral and had left him the next day.

Audrey could see her anguish mirrored in the man's eyes as she looked up. For the first time in months, she didn't feel alone, and the

crushing weight began to lift off her shoulders, if just slightly. She began to believe that maybe she did have a future and that it could be with this man, with his kind hazel eyes, wet with their mutual tears.

They'd come here to end their union, but there was still hope. Audrey stood up and took Burley's side, leading him away from the bar and toward the beech where they had exchanged vows three years before. She would call off the divorce the next day, and they would work on renewing their vows tonight.

The Friendly Next-Door Neighbor

I won't lie to you, I packed it in after my fourth divorce. In my life, there will be no Pare husbands. I am 47 years old, married, and have a successful career. I work as the chief editor of a large book publishing house and live in a condo I bought with the Paney from my second husband's divorce settlement. Okay, so he messed with my young assistant for two years before I realized what was going on, but I made him pay for it. I did very well because he was the CEO of a big trust corporation.

I'm not going to go into detail about my third and fourth husbands. One of them was a mediocre musician. The first lasted seven months, and the second was a politician.

Is there anything else I can say?

It had been five years since then. Dax, my dog, and Pa and Jay, my two cats, now live with me. I can't really tell them apart, but it doesn't matter because they get their meals on time and with a lot of love.

My Soho condo is on 11th Avenue, with views of the Hudson River and New Jersey, but don't laugh; the sunsets are spectacular.

I have friendly neighbors, but I don't see them very much because everyone is still busy in the Big City. A year ago, I had a Chinese couple living next door who was really sweet and imported freshwater pearls from Asia. They made a blunder and moved back to Hong Kong after eight years, and their apartment was now for sale.

I wasn't too impressed with some of the couples who made offers for it. I'm known as "Provincial." What am I to say? Then one day I discovered it had been sold. I thought it was just another couple because there weren't many single men in this house, but it turned out to be a bachelor. Whatever the case, I had no desire to be involved with another guy.

Then, about a week later, I ran into him in the elevator after we both pressed the same floor button. It was a rainy Sunday afternoon after I walked Dax, who detested the rain despite my purchase of a $175 yellow designer raincoat from the Dog Boutique. He looked silly in it and despised it, and I couldn't blame him. I really did not want to deal with wet hair in my home. Normally, I have a dog walker look

after him, but it was Sunday, and we wanted at least one day to get to know each other.

“Can you tell me what kind of dog he is?” The man inquired, a soft smile on his face. I could tell he'd just returned from the local Food store because he was holding a couple of their plastic bags.

“It's a Shelty,” I explained. I said, “A Shetland Sheep Dog or a miniature Collie.”

“He's a real cutie. What is his age?

As the elevator door on our floor opened, I told him, "He's four." In case my daughter decided to visit, I stayed in 8A, a two-bedroom, two-bathroom layout. By the way, his name was Bobby Rocco, and he lived next door in 8B, a one-bedroom apartment with no children who never came to see him.

Anyway, as he walked towards his house, he said, "See you later," which is a traditional greeting. He did, however, come over later to borrow some ground coffee that he said he had forgotten to purchase.

Of course, that trick has been around since women used mortars and pestles to grind their coffee, but it was a Sunday, it was raining, and I was bored, so I invited him in while I was already boiling a pot.

Let's not get ahead of ourselves right now. I wasn't looking for romance or something like that. I was just looking for some business. I'd taken some new author's work home, but I wasn't in the mood to read a horror novel.

He was looking out my big window at New Jersey across the river, which was pretty much fogged in, but he didn't seem to mind. Soon after, the coffee maker beeped, signaling that it was ready, and I asked if he wanted milk and sugar as I poured the dark liquid into a mug that my daughter had given me instead of flowers.

He exclaimed, "Oh, thanks no, no sugar and no milk!" "I used to be in the navy, so I'm used to drinking it black..."

Bobby must have stood at least six feet tall. His hair was shaved cleaned. His stance was that of a Padel, and his face was full of personality. He wasn't likely especially attractive as a young man, but age can help a man stand out. He would have looked great in a uniform as well. He seemed to be in his early fifties, in my opinion.

I just said it because he said he was a navy man and I thought it would be a good conversation starter.

"Well, going through this muck would take a good sailor, but with all the electronics on board a Padern vessel, it would be no problem. Designing navigational equipment is exactly what I do."

We took a seat on my sofa. We sipped our coffee as I tucked my legs under me. He inquired about my background. I inquired about himself. He might have a decent conversation. He'd traveled the globe and had a lot of fascinating stories to share. I considered approaching him about writing a book about it.

We felt as if time had passed us by. I wanted to invite him to dinner but was afraid I'd scare him away. He presumably understood and returned to his apartment after thanking me for the coffee. He had completely forgotten about the ground coffee he had come in for.

I understand your point of view. There she goes, breaking her resolutions if some interesting guy comes along, but you're wrong, I had no such plans, he just seemed like a good boy, which is exactly what you want in a next-door neighbor. There's no way around it.

I returned to work the next day, a dreary Panday. I hadn't finished my homework or read the horror story, and I hadn't had any dreams about Bobby, nor was he on my mind.

Marco, my assistant, was already there and had my schedule planned out for me. I'm done with young and sexy assistants. Marco was a middle-aged gay man with a sharp mind. Columbia University, not the nation, is where I majored in English. He knew exactly where to cross a 'T' and where to position a colon.

I asked him to read the horror novel, and I believe he enjoyed it more than I did. That's how some people are.

The week flew by, and I had no recollection of my next-door neighbor. I see I'll have to clarify that to you very often.

When I got home from work on Friday, however, I saw him exiting the elevator with a young woman. Of course, we exchanged greetings, and he easily introduced her as his niece. I figured I heard him say something to her on their way out that sounded like I was his neighbor. I figured I heard a giggle from her. I despised her.

Dax, Pa, and Jaye greeted me at the entrance, signaling the start of another weekend. I poured myself a glass of red wine and stood there staring at the sunset over New Jersey.

You're beginning to feel sorry for me, I see. Don't do it! I have a full life; in particular, I'm going to a party at the Metropolitan Museum

of Art tomorrow, and yes, I have a date with a wonderful gentleman I've known for years. Okay, he's a distant cousin who'll be in town this weekend, so who cares?

The party was fantastic. The event is held once a year to raise funds for the museum. All of the important people were in attendance, and we raised almost $150,000 to repair the roof of one of the wings.

There was a small band for dancing, and the Met's mezzo-soprano sang a few Puccini arias.

My cousin had a stomach problem about an hour later, so he had to leave early for his hotel, and I took a cab home. It's not a big deal.

It rained again on Sunday, so I locked Dax in the bathroom. We didn't feel like going out. The cats, on the other hand, were unconcerned.

I woke up with Pa and Jay kissing my face because I slept late. I completely forgot to feed them. It was too early for lunch, so I brewed a pot of coffee and turned my gaze back to New Jersey.

Please don't think I want the presence of a man in my home. That is unquestionably a no-no!

My phone rang as I was thinking about that. I hadn't expected anybody, including the dog walker I look after on Thursdays. Maybe there's a FedEx box somewhere, containing a script that someone felt I needed right away.

Bobby, my next-door neighbor, was standing there with a tray wrapped in a napkin and a grin on his face.

He walked straight into the kitchen without so much as an invitation, saying, "I hope I didn't wake you." He slid the tray onto the counter and, with toreador dexterity, yanked the napkin from the tray, yelling "Ole!"

It was a blintzes plate. He said, “Strawberry.” “It's fresh. I just finished making them. I hope you don't have a strawberry allergy...? I smelled some freshly brewed coffee and wondered if you'd like anything to go with it?”

Of course, they were delicious, and Bobby did stay for a while. He said that the girl or woman he was seen with was his niece from Baltimore. I’m hoping for the best. Was it really that important to me?

As a result, we became fast friends. I still don't want to marry again, but it doesn't matter because he lives next door. Can it get any Pare convenient?

The Veil Is Lifted

Daisy returned to the waiting limo, wrapping the mauve jumper around her slender shoulders to keep the evening chill at bay. The driver parted the center window just as she sat down in the plush leather seat, her long legs crossed and champagne in hand. His golden eyes lingered on her black gown and sheer hosiery, appreciatively. For a brief moment, she forgot about Lorenzo and his floozy and indulged in a man's admiration for her fading beauty. Even though the tanned, muscular driver was much too young for her and that she would never cross the line with coworkers, he boosted her libido, which she had declared legally dead.

"Do you want to follow him?" he inquired.

Daisy's lips were drawn together in a tight line. As the limo followed Lorenzo at a safe distance, she simply nodded and fixed her eyes on the resort's immaculate grounds, its sloping, lush landscape and novelty shops rapidly faded from view.

Daisy's dark hole in her heart had once been filled with infinite love before Lorenzo's numerous affairs. She was drawn in by Lorenzo's deceptive charms the moment she gazed into his piercing green eyes, having been shielded by her wealthy father, Wendell Freeman, and her lack of experience with men. They were married six months after meeting each other, despite her father's wishes.

Rumors spread like flames in a small town like New Lisbon, Wisconsin, and it didn't take long for his insatiable taste in women and fine living to be discovered. Lorenzo continued his affairs at Daisy's expense, earning three degrees from the world's top universities, and still having no idea what he wanted to do with his life at the age of fifty-six. What hurt her the most was his inability to have children, which she knew would never happen now that her biological clock had stopped ticking. She loved him through it all.

Daisy, on the other hand, felt nothing but loathsome scorn for her husband tonight as she gazed ahead at the lover's profile against the night sky. Lorenzo was between the woman's thighs, foaming at the mouth, riding her like a dog in heat, oblivious to his sacred marriage vows and the wife who'd given him everything, she imagined. A fresh wave of anger erupted from the depths of her psyche, blinding her with rage and devouring her with vengeance. She shattered the

champagne glass by hurling it into the side window. What right does he have to say that? Who did he think he was, anyway?

Over the intercom, a smooth voice inquired, "Is everything okay?"

Daisy's insides were shaking so violently that she felt sick. She pulled her make-up compact from her purse and powdered her nose with a shaky breath.

She snatched the bottle of champagne from the crushed ice and held it to her lips. The bubbly liquid swished around her mouth, leaving an impression on her mind. When the limo coasted to a stop on a quiet, ominous lane, she tilted the champagne for a second helping, but her entire body went still. Her attention was drawn to Lorenzo's car as she slowly set the bottle aside. Was it her money that was used to buy this house? The impressive, well-kept house, nestled between collages of sugar maple trees, was accessible through an iron gate that parted. Lorenzo pulled into the circular driveway, got out of the driver's seat, and walked over to help the woman out of the vehicle. Before he took her hand and vanished through an arched entrance covered in climbing roses, they shared a private joke and kissed passionately.

Daisy checked her diamond-studded watch after what felt like a lifetime and saw that only an hour had passed. With gloved hands, she tugged at the blonde wig, making sure her chestnut hair didn't fall out.

It had come to an end.

She got out of the limo, walked toward the house, and forced the door open. Her shoes gently tapped against the cobblestones. She opened the gate and was pleased to discover it was unlocked. She rushed to Lorenzo's car, slipping through the tiny gap, and waited.

Lorenzo eventually strode out of the building, whistling, fifteen minutes later. Her heart grew heavier as he got closer, knowing their time together was coming to an end tonight, and it weighed even more, knowing he'd used her in every way possible.

Lorenzo gasped and took a step backward, startled. "What are you doing here, Daisy?"

Given that the scent of a woman's perfume was borne by the wind, Daisy made the only logical inference. "I suppose I should ask you the same question. What are you doing in this place?"

"I'm going to drop off a friend. She had been stranded..."

"Don't insult my intellect, Lorenzo, because we both know she's yet another slut in your lifetime of deception."

His eyes blazed with anger as he stepped toward the motorcycle. "We'll talk about it at home."

Daisy's composure was wearing thin. "You don't have a place to live. All you have is the clothes on your back, and you should be grateful for that." She took a piece of paper and a pen from her pocket. "Sign," she yelled angrily.

He laughed. "Do you really believe I'm that naive? To get rid of me, you'll have to go to great lengths. I'm used to a comfortable lifestyle, and whether we're together or not, I expect it to continue. So, return to your rightful place. I'll be waiting for you there."

"This is your last opportunity. I'll give you a hundred thousand dollars and a peaceful divorce if you sign."

"You're pitiful. No other man would ever be interested in you."

He had never made her dislike him more. "You are right. I'm pathetic for marrying a loser like you. Many men, including the one you call your best friend, are waiting to take your place." She returned the document to her pocket. "My deal has come to an end."

Lorenzo's face was flushed, and his lips were twisted into a menacing snarl. "Harold wouldn't have you because you're a dried-up hag."

"He's already done it." She walked down the street, her feet stomping on the ground. Although she'd lied about sleeping with Harold, Lorenzo's shocked expression made up for the pain he'd caused so quickly.

Lorenzo spoke up from behind her. "This relationship has reached the end of its usefulness. Carol and I, on the other hand, want to be together.

I'll leave quietly for two million dollars." She tried not to pay attention to him, but hearing him refer to the other woman by name broke her heart.

As Lorenzo got into his car, Daisy returned to the limo, casting one last glance over her shoulder at Lorenzo. She told the driver, "Drive to the next block." She took a flat silver gadget from her purse once they were in place. Her finger came to a halt as she pondered her decision one last time. Her humiliation, pain, and rage provided her with the strength she needed. She activated the switch. As a ball of rumbling fire tore through the sky, dispersing into several pockets

of fire and leaving dense smoke in its wake, a deafening explosion shook the calm of the city. The ground under the limo shook, and a streetlight flickered before fully darkening them. The limo accelerated forward.

"Where to?" the driver inquired after a short distance.

Daisy raised her head from her lap, the tremors still reverberating through her body. "It's time to go home. When the cops come to inform me of my husband's misfortune, I want to be in bed."

In the rearview mirror, the driver's eyes met hers, and his words left no space for interpretation. "Do you mind if I console you about your loss after they leave?" Daisy cracked a grin. "It would be fantastic."

The Daughter of the Maid

"Sienna!" exclaims the speaker. Sienna, it's you! Sienna, it's you!" Benjamin slammed the cafe doors shut. As he moved past two people to the counter, every customer's head snapped in his direction. Sienna's boss gave her a cold stare. She lowered her head, blushed slightly, and walked over to where he stood on the last stool.

"Benji!" exclaims the speaker. Benji, it's you! Benji, it's you!" She hissed; her teeth clenched.

Benjamin reached into his coat pocket and took out a small maroon ring box with his hand. With a thud, he set it on the table. Despite the breezy fall weather outside, Sienna found his hands trembling and sweat on his forehead. His smile, on the other hand, never faded. Sienna retrieved a mug for Benjamin's coffee from under the cold metal surface.

"What is this?" She inquired quietly, hoping that people would re-enter their discussions as soon as they had exited them. Sienna set the coffee pot on the table, leaned back on her elbow, and took the box from the counter. Benjamin twitched slightly, as though

reaching out to take it back. When she opened the package, he had to shove his hands in his pockets to keep from doing it again. The setting sun shone brighter through the big windows, highlighting the large princess cut engagement ring. Sienna slammed it against the table. She'd never owned something so valuable before.

Benjamin yelled, catching the box until it shattered on the concrete.

“Is that for Danah, Benji?” she exclaimed.”

“Of course, it's for Danah,” he said, his eyes narrowing in her direction.

“Wow,” she exhaled, resuming her grip on the coffee pot, “I didn't realize you two were serious.”

“What exactly does that imply?” “Benjamin put the ring box back into his coat pocket. He leaned forward and put his glasses into place.

“There isn't anything. Do you believe she'll accept? Sienna made her way down the counter, refilling the empty cups.

“Yes,” says the speaker.

“When are you going to ask her?”

“The semester is coming to a close.”

“Can you tell me why you've been waiting so long?”

As he stood, following her path around the tiny cafe, he objected, "It's just a few months."

“My brother couldn't even wait an hour when he bought the ring. In the grocery store, he asked Katie.”

Benjamin scoffed, “I’m not going to propose to Danah in a grocery store.”

“Benji, it was romantic. Sienna grumbled, "He couldn't wait to spend the rest of his life with her."

“Didn't they split up before the wedding?” you may wonder.” Sienna turned around a furious expression on her face. Her eyes narrowed and her nose scrunched up.

“How come you're still here?”

"Because I’m in desperate need of my best friend right now."

“I love you, but I have to go to work. What's more, don't you have any sense of decency? “No, no,” Sienna said, her gaze shifting from

Benjamin to the wall clock. "No!" he exclaimed as he returned his gaze. "I'll call you later?" he says, turning back to Sienna."

"I leave at seven o'clock."

He repeated the number seven to himself, then dashed towards the entrance, pulling his coat tighter around his neck.

"They'll kick you out if you're late again!" She chased him down.

"I'm going to Yale!"

"That'll teach them a lesson!"

"And it'll irritate my father to no end!" Before speeding down the highway, Benjamin flashed her a devilish smile.

Benjamin dashed through the throngs of people on the streets, weaving in and out of cars as he attempted to cross the street. When he bounded on, he could hear the campus bells ringing out the time. He hadn't seen the young woman walking straight at him because his gaze was fixed on the brick hall he was approaching. The two students collided with a clash of heads, causing both to crash to the ground and Benjamin to slip backward. He felt a sudden pain in his brain. An aftershock of the impact ripped through his chest with a low grumble.

"Where in the world are you running to, Benjamin?" "What is this?" Danah asked from above him." she inquired. Benji's gaze was drawn to the maroon box that had landed on the cement beside him after falling from his coat. Danah knelt, but Benjamin grabbed it from her clutches and hoped she would forget about it. For a brief moment, he tried to get his feet under him. Danah reached out and assisted him in getting to his feet. Benjamin backed away with a flinch. "What's the matter with you?" She chuckled.

"Nothing," he said quickly, "I have to get to class." Before continuing his run, Benjamin kissed her on the lips hurriedly. As he went, her short blonde hair blew up in her face, like something out of a film.

Danah screamed, "I love you," but he did not hear her.

At 7:00 p.m., Benjamin waited outside the cafe. The sun had begun to set, casting a golden glow on everything that was about to die. He thought it was ironic that the metallic gleam could shine on those who couldn't enjoy it. He waited for Sienna while rolling the ring box in his hand and leaning against the glass.

"Good evening, Mr. Brants," she said, pulling at her brown curls and wrapping a red scarf around her waist. "How are the misses doing?"

When she left, Sienna took the ring box from his hands and said, "She's always a miss."

She opened the package to admire the ring and exclaimed, "I can't believe you're going to ask Danah to marry you." “I recall when you used to think she was a jerk.”

“People evolve.”

“Didn't you, do it?” She made a snide remark. Sienna cautiously put the ring on her finger.

“I happen to like her,” Benjamin said as he took Sienna's ring and put it back in his pocket.

“You shouldn't be carrying that around.”

“And she loves me,” he said, oblivious to her.

“It also helps that you two have been groomed to be together since birth,” Sienna sighed, her hair flipping. Benjamin locked his gaze on her. “Oh, come on,” she rolled her eyes. Tell me your parents haven't been trying to get you married to Danah Black since you were able to walk.”

“I don't always follow my parents' instructions.”

"Are you serious? You applied to Harvard because of them," Sienna scoffed. "Because of them, you're learning mathematics. Because of them, you started dating Danah."

"I don't do what my parents tell me to," he said again, his teeth clenched.

"Think about one thing-"

"Didn't I remain friends with you?" He yelled angrily. "What is this all about?" he asked as he came to a halt."

"What are you talking about?" Sienna peered around his back to see her friend standing still in a bookstore's glare. "What are you doing?"

"Don't you despise her?"

"I don't despise her-"

"But you do," he said angrily. "You start in on me, her, or my parents every time I bring her up."

"Your parents, Benji-"

He said, "I love her."

"Benji"

"I adore her, and I want you to enjoy her as well. Since I adore her, I want you to be able to see her in all of her glory."

"Could you please refrain from saying that?" Sienna muttered under her breath. She combed her hair with her chipped fingernails. Sienna surrendered herself to the shadows as darkness fell over the town like a blanket, keeping everyone cold. "I don't despise Danah in the least. I despise the fact that she is the one you chose. I've always thought..." she trailed off, her back to Benjamin.

"What are you talking about?" What did you predict would happen?" He walked over to her and saluted her.

"Do you recall the old treehouse in your backyard? "We used to eat the sandwiches my mother made as she washed, our legs hanging off the edge, the way your father despised it," she said, her back to him. Do you recall our strategy?"

Benjamin came to a halt about a foot away from her. Her arms were folded over her stomach. He couldn't see her face, but he could see her shoulders shiver as tears streamed down her cheeks. He wanted to reach out and touch her shoulder, telling her that he would never forget her. He decided to remind her that he could still recall the distance between Lawrence and Los Angeles. But it was all just a

child's fantasy, set to happen on an ideal day—tomorrow, a day that would never come.

"All you had to do was submit, didn't you?" Finally, Sienna turned around. "And where does that leave me?"

"Sienna," she says.

"And then it was Danah this and Danah that, and here I am, standing behind the same counter I'll be standing behind until I die, and the only person who held me going-" she paused, trembling, "I can still remember making fun of Danah." I recall you resenting the money and vowing to survive without it. Anything you're trying to forget is still fresh in my mind. You used to make jokes about Danah-"

"Who was I meant to marry, huh?" Benjamin flailed his arms to the left. "Who?" he demanded, rage coursing through his veins. Is it the daughter of a maid?" He spited in Sienna's face the words.

She shivered and sank deeper into the darkness of the night. Her tears had left a stain on her cheeks. Her lips trembled. Benjamin drew his arms down to his sides. He hadn't said that in jest. He wished to start over, so he closed his eyes. And everything she said was real, not just that night, but from the beginning. This is so painfully true.

He did, however, adore Danah.

He loved her.

He was smitten by her.

Thank you, God! He wished he didn't have to keep reminding himself to say it.

She was gone when he opened his eyes again.

"Benjamin?" He jerked his head to the sound of her voice.

"Danah?" I inquire.

She took a step forward into the sunlight. In the neon buzz of the bookstore sign, her blonde hair was almost white. She drew back her perfectly painted lips to expose a toothy grin. Benjamin rubbed his hand across his forehead, attempting to awaken from the nightmare he had become engrossed in.

"What are you doing out here?"

"I was talking to a friend," Benjamin said, turning to look for Sienna once more as if she'd reappeared as soon as she had disappeared.

He shut his eyes and wished as much as he could, but the same night air blew at his back. How could he have made such a blunder? The daughter of a cleaner. Who did he imagine himself to be? Benjamin

reached up and gently tugged on the ends of his hair with his fingertips. Danah approached him, her arms around his waist and her head resting on his shoulder. Benjamin was startled and bolted backward. Her touch pricked him in the stomach and ran up his spine like thorns. He let everything wash away as he turned to face her. What made him think he loved Danah? She gave a warm smile. It didn't mean anything. It was insignificant.

"What's the matter?" She enquired; her eyes narrowed. If he stayed, she'd be staring at him for the rest of his life. There was nothing as Danah took his hand in hers. "I adore you."

He admitted that he had let other people's views take the place of his own. Danah was not someone he adored. He had no feelings for her. He was, however, terrified. I'm terrified. It was simply easier to follow orders rather than think for himself. All of it had come to a halt because his own personal feelings had gotten in the way. But they returned at that moment, on that sidewalk, in the store's sun. It seemed abrupt and all at once, but it wasn't. He had always loved Sienna, but it was only then that he realized. He obviously adored her. It was, without a doubt, her

Danah said it again, "I love you." He replied, "I love her."

My Best Friend

"What!"

This simple word had her reeling. She knew the reason why they were even there now was that she still cared about him, but he did not know how much, at the point that she'd been unable to have lasting relationships with other men because her feelings for him left her so humbled. The desire inside her to shout that he was the love of her life could not resist, always had been, and always would be.

She really wanted to say to him these exact words looking into his eyes: "I know what you mean, and I guess what you must be thinking. You were right all along. Believe me, I tried to make things work with other men. It felt so different just being in the arms of another man more than once, but I just could not keep faking it. I eventually just gave up when I realized I always found something wrong with other men simply because they didn't have your smile or your laugh, or they weren't as chivalrous as you."

Instead, she shrugged. "I just got tired of being in pointless relationships." And simply left the room. He did not stop her.

"What's happened? You are so strange recently." Her mother said extremely disappointed.

"This is nothing. Don't worry." She replied avoiding eye contact.

"I know there is something wrong with you. I'm your mum I feel it." Her mother said kindly.

"Really it is nothing. I am super fine. Don't worry!!" She said loudly and opened the yogurt to eat it.

"Oh, my lovesick baby!" Her mother said trying to understand her daughter's concern.

"Shut up!" She grew irate. She left the yogurt on the table and left the room.

Furthermore, she could not stop thinking about him. Every time someone wanted to ask about how she was feeling or something more than usual, she got very irritated out of the blue. She hates herself for that. She has been terribly busy with her work in the last week, and that was true, but she was also so confused every time she

met David, her school's best friend. As her mother pointed out she found herself getting upset over nothing.

After a few minutes, her mother suddenly came into her room. It was humiliating, but Fiona made a pathetic pleading gesture with her hands. "Mum you know how much I love David. I am sure he is into Jessica. I could never be as skinny and pretty as her."

"My deepest apologies. I think I took her for my sweet Fiona, the girl who is proud of herself and has the nerve to speak in public." She sighed dramatically. "Sorry, mum. I feel upset and I do not know how to confess my feeling for him.

"Baby, there is something I want to tell you. There are many types of relationships out there. An acquaintance could simply be someone you may have a conversation with and may have a few drinks with like a colleague. So, they are not going to be someone you talk to whenever you are feeling down about yourself or need a shoulder to cry on. Friendship and love might be often misinterpreted. Both friendship and love are a form of connection that has one giant trait that makes them closer than you think: intimacy, which is the emotional connection you feel with someone and makes the difference between a friend and acquaintances. I believe a friend is

someone you want to be around as often as possible. You call a friend a person that you can be open your feelings to, and they are a person you can stay a long time with and never get bored or tired of them. Love and friendship both share this intimacy. Do not forget that the line between love and friendship is difficult to draw, and it is also true that a romantic relationship is not going to last if there is no intimate connection. This is the main reason why a lot of couples fall in love with their best friend. Friendship is a form of love, baby. Respect and affect are the most important factors in a true friendship. However, love and especially true love involves commitment and intimacy, which friendships can have, but also involves a romantic attraction. You should feel sexually attracted to this person. If they do not make the butterflies in your stomach go wild, and they release chemicals in your brain that make you want to do anything for them. This is not a sign of love.

I know a friend who thought she fall for his best friend. But after their passion goes down, after the honeymoon stage, they decided to break up losing the most important person.

What you have to remember is the importance of commitment, which is quite important in a romantic relationship, more than anything else. Despite friendship may have some form of

commitment. Often, you can share some goals that you want to accomplish with your friend. With that said, commitment does not necessarily need to be there for a great friendship. In fact, you can have some friends who live entirely different lives, for example abroad, but still find the time to talk to each other and catch up.

The passion that platonic friends have may dwindle over time, or it may become bottled up to the point of explosion, Fiona. You may always wonder what could have been. If you do not take a risk and tell your best friend how you feel, you will never know if they felt the same way. You may watch them go off with another partner and yearn for the romantic relationship you could have had with them. Of course, it is ultimately your choice to tell him how you feel, but you may go through life with regrets if you don't confess your feelings.

It is not strange that a romance can start as a great friendship. And you and David have been friends for a long time, which may make it harder to transition to a relationship. If he loves you, I guess he sees you as a good friend and does not want to lose you by transitioning into something more fragile. But if not admitting your feelings can mess you up so much, Fiona, well I want you to confess your love for David. I am with you. I am also sure you will find a

good moment to confess your love. Just go and ask him instead of building castles in the air." Her mother smile weakly and left the room.

She did not really want to tell him the truth, but she knew he was relentless if he thought someone was lying to him. She was decided to ask him something about her just to break the ice and then say something like "You are my rock! I would be lost without you. What can I do without you?" or something like that which could be signs of a deep connection. At that moment she received a confirmation message from David.

"What are you thinking right now?" Her gaze snapped to his face as he leaned back in his chair, studying her with piercing eyes the color of rich turquoise. "That maybe we should have gone out for dinner after all." She smiled weakly.

He arched a single brow. "Why did you ask me out?" She released a jagged breath, hoping he would not be too put off by her honesty. "Because I have to confess that you are such an important person for me. It is hard to ignore this thing. You have been with me since elementary school and you always support me, not only at work but in my struggles even when I lost my father in that terrible incident. Your presence is so important to me, and I cannot ignore this

whatever it is. What you have been made for me in all these years is priceless.

He quirked his lips into a lopsided grin and spoke. "This thing? That is what you're calling it?"

"What do you mean? What else should I call it?"

"How about friendship?" he said quietly as he stood to his feet. Fiona's heart plunged to her stomach as she followed him with her eyes. She thought he would cross the length of the table toward her, but instead, he walked in front of her.

"When I saw your message, I wondered what I would say to you. I was thinking the same thing. I needed to talk to you so long ago." he spun around then to pin her with his gaze. "I wondered if what we felt toward each other all those years ago was still there and if it was then what would it mean." She stood to her feet and on shaky legs slowly crossed the room toward him, dinner long forgotten. It scared her to realize just how in sync she and David truly were.

His words echoed the thoughts that had raced through her head when she decided to take his hand. What she felt for him all those

years ago had not been imagined but was it still there and now was even grown, and if it was then she too wondered what it meant.

"And tell me, honestly what do you think it means?" She asked softly. "Well, it is obvious that we like each other, and we're attracted to each other." He settled his hands against her shoulders and pulled her closer to him, so close that he could hear her next breath caught in her chest as she waited for him to speak. "I think you know what it means, the question now is what do we do about it?" She tilted her head back to meet his gaze and knew that the conflicting emotions that crossed his face were mirrored on her own.

"I want this, David. I am not just talking about calling you in the middle of the night."

"I want that too, but..." She silenced him with a single finger to his lips. He frowned down at her and tried to set her away from him, his eyes full of disappointment, and said: "I am deadly afraid of ruining things between us." You said that before and what did I tell you then?"

"Fiona, I am not going to let you walk away from me again. This time I am standing in front of you, and I want to give you all of me, but you have to know that what you are asking for is very difficult for

me too. But I believe in us. We can be a great couple. I love you. I always loved you, Fiona. I want your happiness more than mine. I wanted to confess my love earlier but there was that terrible accident, and I did not want to make you upset. You needed your time to mourn the loss of your father. I want to protect you. You are my real and only best friend. You are my rock, the reason why I wake up every morning. I cannot live without you or imaging my life without you. I want to stay with you forever. I want to marry you, Fiona. You are the love of my life!"

She could not believe her ears. She was thinking the same things. They were both so stupid.

"Why didn't you tell me before? I... I am speechless. I had no idea that even you… I love you so much, David. You are my love. I cannot live without you. I do not need to wait for my answer I would be honored to become your wife, David, my David." She said while she was crying.

"Sorry if it took me so much time to reach you, Fiona. I did not want to ruin our relationship. But now I am on cloud nine. You do not have any idea about how happy I am right now. I can go out and

said that you are mine. I want to scream that out!" he whispered with a glint in his eye.

"David, please! We are in a restaurant!" she said looking away she felt so embarrassed.

"You are even prettier when you blush." David said with a sweet wide smile. He was so full of love and affection. He kissed her tenderly to calm his attraction.

"I do not want to let you go away. I will do my best to respect and love you for the rest of my life. I do promise it, Fiona. I think we can get married this summer. Tomorrow let's talk to our boss and colleagues." He said proudly.

"Oh my God! I forgot about our colleagues for a second. What should they say? It is okay to have a relationship in the office" She frowned.

"Who cares? I must confess to you that John knew my feeling for you. So, I am quite sure he would be happy to know we are going to get married." He reassured her.

"John is very great. We can trust him." She said relieved.

"Exactly. He is a close friend of mine. No worries. I will speak to him and our boss as well." He replied and kissed her forehead softly.

He sat down again, and they enjoyed delicious Italian food. He paid the bill and drove her home.

He kissed her again with passion in front of the car and he did not want to let her go. He kept smiling and was so glad to have her in his arms so close to her.

"I want to stay with you" She whispered to him many times. "You made me happy. We had the same fear but now we can be truly happy as long as we are together. Please find a place where you would like to hold our marriage ceremony." David asked. He was staring into her eyes so intensely that she blushed again.

"All right. I have an idea. As we both love nature, maybe we should reserve a room near the lake where we went some years ago. I think it would be very romantic, especially when the sun goes down. I do not need a lot of people. Just the one we love. Our families and some close friends, what do you think, honey?" She took courage and said that to him.

He smiled back at her. She felt a shiver down her spine. Her dream to spend the rest of her life with his best friend, the love of her life, finally came true. She felt like she was a child again. She could not sleep that night and kept thinking about David, all the wedding preparations, and the reaction of all the people they knew.

A Need to Depart

She needed to flee. It wasn't the best of times, but when was it ever? Her seven-year boyfriend proposed last month, and she accepted. They got together in one of Marist College's dining halls. He was a sophomore, and she was a junior. There might have been a light drizzle outside that afternoon. They've been together since that fateful day. They were content in each other's company, but their relationship was unremarkable. Did she have feelings for him? She was aware that she was kind to her.

Her supervisor, a lovely mid-thirties lady, had turned down her last-minute offer for a week off. What a scumbag. Not to be deterred, she purchased her ticket to Amsterdam with money set aside for the wedding by her and her fiancé. He was taken aback by her desire to get away for a week, but he embraced her decision regardless. So considerate. She conveniently forgot to tell him that the plane ticket she purchased was only one-way. But, oh well.

Three months later, she snorts a line of coke she got from the bad guy with a lady she met at the same club a week before in a bathroom

stall at De Club in Amsterdam. Because of their degree of intoxication, neither she nor her newfound friend can read the message written in black magic marker on the stall door, even though her Dutch is adequate. She's been doing a lot of cocaine in the last month and has lost weight as a result. The bathroom floor is shaken by the resident DJ's house music. She's scheduled to board a plane back to the United States in six hours, but she's not worried about that right now. If she doesn't get it, she doesn't get it. Last month, and the month before that, the same thing happened. When her friend requests toilet paper, she takes a roll from her bag. It's still useful. They argue over where they should go next as she wipes. Her friend has spent the whole night grinding up some rando and has requested that they return to his flat. She makes it clear that she does not want to be the third wheel. A woman wearing six-inch stilettos slams the stall door and shouts at them to hurry up. What a scumbag. They tell her to get out of here.

And with the music blaring, they can both hear that one of the two-bathroom sinks has been left running. She's feeling fine thanks to the coke line, and she has no plans to leave the club anytime soon. Besides, she looks great in the lavender dress she borrowed from a friend who is now standing beside her. A street vendor selling

herring can be found outside. Amid all the shouting and commotion in the bathroom, they both remember how amusing their current situation is, each doing bumps while the other pees. They laugh so loudly that it can be heard by the ladies in the other stalls. They hug for a long time and then help each other clean the residue off their noses with toilet paper. The twosome plan to meet in the bathroom after another hour on the dance floor, now that they've washed up. The bitch in stilettos is banging on the stall door once more. When they leave the stall, they exchange words. She realizes the bathroom is dimly lit red for the first time. That would be the only thing she remembered that night, as the remainder of the night passed her by in a blur.

She awoke on the futon of that rando's third-floor flat at 3 p.m. the next day. The flight was canceled. But, oh well. She realized she had remained loyal to her fiancé because she was still wearing the lavender dress. They communicated by email. He sent one every day, and she answered once a week. It seemed strange to her that he had so much to say and she had so little, although she was the one traveling the globe and he was trapped in his everyday routine at home. Down below, three kids could be heard kicking a soccer ball. Will she be willing to marry him? Yeah, she would marry him until

her money ran out and there were no more couches to sleep on. She pondered why she kept putting back her return date as she sat drowsily in front of the living room window. Although the response was self-evident, speaking it out loud was not. Saying it to him in person would be even more difficult. How could she tell her fiancé that she felt more alive in a bathroom stall with a stranger than she had in the six years she had spent with him?

She lay silently on the futon, looking at the crack in the ceiling. Is it true that it rained the day they met at Marist? She can't seem to remember anything.

The Obsession

They say hindsight is 20/20, but I'm not in the market for it. I'm well aware that I'm engulfed in an obsession, one marked by dark eyes, full lips, and hands that make my resolve crumble. Except for the odd late-night evening, which I'm sure I'll be available for, he's still busy. He has a tiny apartment, a soul-sucking day job, a mind full of desire, and an epic chip on his shoulder that he doesn't have. There is no space in his life for me; well, I think there is a tiny amount of room he creates from time to time, and I oblige, but with a gnawing desire for more.

I'll be there. We'll sit on his sofa, he'll be dressed down, and he'll give me wine. He'll then kiss me, and I'll kiss him again. We'll continue our conversation over a second glass of wine. Before the conversation comes to a close, he'll kiss me again, and I'll moan into his mouth. We'll leave his couch and make our way to his room. In between urgent kisses, he'll undress and then me. We're going to fuck. It'll be fantastic. I'm not sure if I'm going to cum.

We'll lie in his room, naked, exhausted, and out of breath. We'll continue our conversation. Then he'll fuck me some more. He'll ask me what I want, and I'll have no idea what to say. I have very little sexual experience and shy temperament, the extent of which isn't completely clear to him. He'll do it.

We'll chat some more, and I'll hope he'll invite me to stay, but he won't. So, when I pick up my clothes strewn around his bedroom floor, my heart will sink a little. I'll get dressed and tell myself it'll be fine. I'm not planning on staying the night. It makes no difference.

He'll take me to my car on foot. I'm going to kiss him again, this time with my palms on his face and his on my waist. It will be about one o'clock in the morning. I'll be home before two o'clock. I'm not going to be tired. I'll be second-guessing myself the whole evening, wondering what I'm doing and when I'll stop.

Join me in my escape.

He said, "Run away with me." I opened my eyes and blinked. "Let's run away and get married," says one of them.

I'm married. It didn't come as a surprise, but it still sounded strange and forbidden.

“However, we are unable to do so. I half believed it when he said, "We can't just go and..." What would we do if we left? What would we do if this happened? What do you think they'd say?

“Of course, we can,” Who is going to put a stop to us?” He smiled determinedly as if he were a child.

He reached for my hand as he moved closer. The feelings I harbored for him rushed through me, exhilarating and satisfying. Isn't it certain that this will never change?

“Take a look. You won't be able to convince me otherwise.”

“What about my family...?”

“They adore you, and I adore you. They'll figure it out.”

I backed away and sat down on my bunk, dreading the possibility of defiance.

“However, where will we go?”

“I’m not sure. Dalleen Green, anyone?” He took a seat next to me.

“That is so self-evident. And a little tacky,” I said as I pressed my hand against his thigh, feeling the curved edge of his kneecap through his trousers. I adored his slender legs.

"We'll go wherever you want," How about a trip to Bath? You said you enjoyed your time there."

When I was still living at home, I went with my family a few years ago.

"It's true. "Bath is lovely."

"Then that's where we'll go,"

"How are we going to get there?"

"We'll catch the first train out of town the next morning."

I looked down at my gold watch, which my sister had given me for my eighteenth birthday.

it's your birthday "It's already tomorrow morning,"

"That's even better!" He got to his feet. "I'll call a taxi for us to get to the station. We'll stay in the greasy spoon across the street for the rest of the night. We'll eat bacon butties and drink tea before our train arrives," says the group.

"And where are we going to stay in Bath?"

"I'm staying in a hotel. We'll stay in the biggest, most luxurious hotel we can find,"

"No, Johnny..." says the speaker.

"It's true. "It's my pleasure," he said, putting me out of my misery. Everyone was talking about how wealthy he was, but only I knew for sure.

"All right."

He said, "I'll be back," and then walked away.

I inhaled deeply and pulled my cardigan around my shoulders. It was nice and smelled like my perfume because it was made of pure merino wool. Lucy next door, Debbie across the street, and Georgie down the hall came to mind. They were most likely all sleeping soundly or watching TV in their rooms this late at night. I wanted to tell them – to express my outrage and joy – but I was afraid of their reaction. On our corridor, eloping to marry wasn't something that happened every day.

Johnny always said I was too concerned about what other people think of me, but that didn't stop me from being ecstatic about him and us. I thrived on our late-night sessions, which required me to cross corridors and use gentle, covert knocks. I was aware that they

spoke about us; we weren't as inconspicuous or invisible as we thought, but that didn't deter me.

I opened my closet and looked at my clothes; there were so many fresh and unworn items, so many that were too big or too small. When we return, I should have a clean house.

Are you planning to return? That had not occurred to me. When we get back, I should have asked him what happens next. It was the most crucial issue, and neither of us had given it any thought. With a shake of my head, I forced the thought to the back of my mind. I told myself that I had permission to be happy. That was something I was getting pretty good at.

"What does a bride-to-be wear on her wedding day, you might wonder." I said, putting on a silly accent, to the wardrobe. It responded by directing my attention to a pale pink summer dress with a floaty hem that danced in the gentlest breezes. While it wasn't quite summering yet, I was hoping for some sunshine.

I had a bag packed in a matter of seconds. A gentle tap on the door revealed him, dressed in a grey three-piece suit with a too-tight tie knot. I'd never seen him dressed like this before, and it reminded me of his unpredictable nature. I admired how he saw life as a series of

large parties, each with its own outfit. At his feet was an old brown suitcase. These days, no one carries suitcases like that. I admired him for being special.

I gave him a firm kiss on the mouth. It seemed like the beginning of something.

"Let's go," I said quietly.

We sat in large, upright chairs after he paid for First Class tickets. A middle-aged man with a briefcase sat across from us, giving us an awkward look before opening a laptop and typing away with few interruptions. I slid my hand under my future husband's and dozed off.

Bath was even more lovely than I remembered. Buildings were higher, hills were steeper, and streets were longer. I used to believe that when I got older, everything got smaller. It felt good to be proven wrong for once.

Our hotel was much more luxurious than I had imagined. I couldn't contribute much to our adventure because I didn't have much income. Nonetheless, I squealed as he jumped onto the giant bed and bounced into me, and I grinned foolishly as I stroked the plump

white towels folded in our bathroom. How could we possibly return to sharing my single bed?

I didn't inquire as to how long we would be staying, but as he drew me closer to him, his bond already loosening, I wished for an eternity.

That afternoon, we gave notice of our impending marriage. The affirmation creased around my fingers as I clutched it so tightly.

It was a mixed bag of joy.

We had to remain in the city for seven days before they agreed to marry us. And we had to wait fifteen days for the notice to be posted in the Registry Office before we could legally marry. They were bureaucratic annoyances that reminded me of the real world and caused me to reconsider all. I inquired as to whether it was worthwhile. Is there a charge for the hotel room? What about those who will miss and be concerned about us? Can they try to track us down? What would we think if that happened? What can we say to them? So, what's next?

He calmed my worries by making plans for us to wait – new clothing, a backgammon board, and a deck of cards. I made a series of false phone calls to Debbie and home, claiming I'd gone on an

unplanned creative writing retreat and couldn't be contacted on my room phone. I don't have to be concerned; Johnny was right...

In those fifteen days, I heard that Johnny liked to sing Frank Sinatra in the bathroom, that he flossed every day, and that before turning off the lamp, he drank half an inch of whiskey in bed. We were slow to get out of bed in the mornings but easy to make sure we didn't miss breakfast. I saw England's endless green dissolve into cities I'd never seen before: Taunton, Bristol, and Weston-super-Mare on days when we took the train further west. We started spending most afternoons walking around Bath hand in hand, always ending up in the tearoom I remembered from my first visit. We became acquainted with the proprietor, Darby, a stout woman dressed in mismatched floral prints and turquoise eye shadow. We told her our secret, and she dubbed us "young lovers," pushing free cake on us at every visit. I was worried that my dress wouldn't suit.

It did, however. It happened when the day came.

One witness was Darby, and the other was our hotel's receptionist. Justyna was a young Polish woman with cat-like green eyes that were almost oval in shape. Her hair was pulled back into an extremely high ponytail, which I didn't like, but she still smiled at us

at the reception desk. She admitted that she, too, had eloped to marry when she was 17 and he was 19. They'd recently marked their fifteenth wedding anniversary. In our restaurant, her husband worked as a chef. We had the impression that she knew, and she took the morning off from work to be with us.

We were to be married at 11:00 a.m., and the air outside was crisp and calm as we walked from the hotel to the Registry Office in a taxi. I wrapped the shawl around my shoulders and buttoned up my favorite cardigan. I'd purchased a new lipstick to match my dress, and when I saw myself in a tiny pocket mirror, I vowed to wear it every day of our marriage. Justyna had taken some white chrysanthemums from the hotel restaurant's dining tables and handed them to me in a bunch of five. I pinned another to the lapel of Johnny's three-piece suit with trembling palms.

The flowers brought it to life. I felt like a real bride as soon as I was holding their long, thin stems in my hands and walking down a short, carpeted aisle. I put my doubts aside and concentrated on the vows I was writing, feeling wonderfully responsible. And, like a balloon about to burst, I felt a huge, exciting pleasure fill me up when Johnny's voice cracked as he said his vows to me. When Johnny took my hand in his and we walked away as husband and wife, the simple

gold bands we'd chosen were similar in every way except size, and the metal was still warm to my skin.

When we went outside, the sun was shining brightly, and Justyna took a picture of us with her phone.

She promised, "I'll give it to you." I didn't even think to ask how. I wasn't questioning anything; I was just living.

Darby said, "You both look so happy," and she stretched out her arms to embrace us.

We went back to the tearoom to toast our witnesses. Champagne, tea, and cakes awaited us on a table topped with a gleaming silver balloon. It said, "Just Married," and we were.

"Congratulations, Mrs. Malcolm," says the speaker.

Our glasses chimed together as we said, "Congratulations, Mr. Malcolm." "It's hard for me to believe we did it."

"What is it like to be married?"

I recalled seeing him for the first time on the day I moved in. I was completely out of place. Isn't it true that I was too young to be there? I saw a glint of dissent in Johnny's eyes as he opened the door for me

to walk down the hallway. He knocked on my door that evening while I was unpacking. As a welcoming present, he'd brought a potted pink orchid and a bottle of Merlot. I invited him to come in and play backgammon with me.

"It feels fantastic. It's incredible. You've been naughty. "Excellent." I lowered my gaze to my ring. "However, I don't think this one will last as long as my first."

He took my married hand in his and covered it with his. "I sincerely hope not. You should note that I am 82 years old."

"We'll see what happens," I said, not feeling a day over eighty-five.

Lifetime Perfume

"Where are you going?"

Grace glanced up from packing his clothes as Andrew ambled into her room dripping wet from his shower with a towel slung low on his hips.

"That's what I was trying to tell you last night, this morning, and as soon as we got back here, but you always have a way of distracting me," she said with a big smile on her face before she turned her attention back to packing.

"Since I only have two appointments in the morning today, I was planning to take a flight back." He crossed the room to stand beside her and he frowned saying: "Why?" She turned her full attention to him after she pushed down on the suitcase until it clicked shut. "Well, as I told you before I have an important meeting in a few days, and I have to prepare my presentation. I was glad we could spend last evening together." She felt he was disappointed, and it tugged at her heart more than she wanted it to. She just had to remind herself

that she was a girl having a grown-up affair. She knew what she'd gotten herself into from the beginning. For him, this is just about sex, and nothing else, she chanted to herself. She forced herself to repeat over and over in her head, hoping it would stick—hoping that she didn't carry around this weight in her heart when she watched that beautiful man moves on to his next conquest.

"I wish I could stay. I've really enjoyed our time together, but now it's time to get back to the real world," she said with a small smile. He just nodded. Later she would realize that she was such a fool, but she just didn't know anything about having affairs, so she wasn't exactly the best when it came to rules about what to say and what not to say. A storm of conflicting emotions swirled inside her at the hard look on his face. She wanted to explain to him so many things, but then that would mean she'd have to admit her flaws. She keeps saying to herself that he enjoyed having flings, but that was it. She felt frustrated so she said loudly "Look, I understand how this works, Andrew. I know when we get back to work it will be business as usual. We're both adults, we had an affair and that's that." Her speech made her sound sophisticated and worldly, so she was immensely proud of it. After all, she did this regularly. "I see." That was all he said. His face was as empty as a blank canvas, devoid of

any expression. He was a man of a few words, but he knew how to express himself authentically.

“I wish you would say something more."

“What else is there to say? You seem to have everything under control.” She was confused as she heard the hard edge in his voice. She didn’t have time now to figure out what was going on in Andrew’s head. She had a plane to catch.

“I don’t know what your problem is. I would think you’d be grateful I wasn’t trying to read more into this.”

“How nice of you,” he said tightly and then he grabbed his clothes and stalked toward the door. She was even more confused she had no idea of what was bugging him, but she hated that he was leaving angry, especially after what they’d shared until that moment.

A voice inside her said: How had she been so wrong about a man she’d seen every time she could for the last two years and a half? She probably didn’t want to see him as anything other than a wild playboy, a voice screamed in her head. She knew that voice was right, and she felt one hundred times worse because of it.

If she felt this bad, she could only imagine what Andrew was going through. She was thirty-six years old and yet she'd never felt more foolish in her entire life. Reaching for her phone, she tried to dial his cell but wasn't surprised when it went straight to voicemail. She then suddenly realized that he may want to see her reaction and an apology too.

Andrew went out on a limb, and she realized she left him hanging. It took her a few minutes to figure out what she had to do, but as soon as she did, she didn't hesitate. Shooting to her feet, she called Andrew again and this time she left a message: I want to see you. I have something to say. She reached his office that wasn't so far from that hotel.

"I'm trying to apologize and seduce you all at once," she said with a naughty smile when she jumped into him at the entrance.

"You smell so good. I see you got it," he said flatly as he frowned. She nodded slowly. "I did. Thank you. It's lovely," she said with a small smile.

"It is your favorite" He added, as he tried to justify why he'd gone to such lengths to impress a woman who apparently still saw what she wanted to see and not what was actually in front of her.

"I'm sorry, Andrew," she said softly. "I don't know how you say now that I'm in front of you. When it comes to men, I don't trust easily, you know." He wanted to say he knew that better than most, but he kept his mouth shut as he just listened.

"Especially when it comes to men who are as attractive and confident as you." As soon as she said that she lowered her gaze to the floor.

"I just didn't believe a man like you would seriously be interested in a woman like me," she barely whispered while keeping her eyes glued to her feet.

He wanted to pummel whoever had convinced her she wasn't beautiful or smart enough for this word because she now seemed to believe it. He swore softly as he dragged her into his arms. He'd caught glimpses of this before—the insecurities that she carried around. She was tall and curvaceous, and she also boasted the most perfect features, with her alluring almond-shaped eyes, pretty heart-shaped face, and full sensual mouth. He'd been captivated the day he'd met her, and it had taken him a while to realize she didn't see herself the way he did. Sticking out a single finger, he lifted her chin until she met his gaze.

"Listen, you're beautiful. I've told you this many times before, as well as shown you with my actions." She smiled.

"I know, I know." She said reaching up a hand to stroke his stubbled jaw. "I'm so sorry it took me so long to see you for the splendid man you really are and not the man I pointed you out to be. Please just give me the chance to show you that I see you for who you truly are. Even if I know I don't deserve it."

"You always find ways to show me how you feel." She said in a hushed whisper. He placed a single finger against her lips to keep her from babbling, something she only did when she was extremely nervous. He understood her anxious expression, but if she truly knew just how long he'd been half in love with her, she wouldn't have been the slightest bit worried about his answer.

"Yes, I'd been angry with the way things had turned out." He replied. He'd planned to return home, lick his wounds and start fresh on Monday with her. He knew when he'd started down this path that going after her wouldn't be easy, but then nothing truly worth having was ever easy to come by.

Her eyes twinkled as red splotches bloomed in her cheeks. "I love you so much I can't stop this feeling." she purred softly as he backed

her toward the desk and she coiled one leg around his calf. "Among many, many other things," he whispered before he dipped his head to capture her lips in a long sensual kiss.

"I love you more. I loved you from the first time I saw you. This is the beginning of a lifetime," he said and then he lowered his head to press a gentle kiss against her soft lips as he gave himself over to the power of their passion, cherishing the thought that this was indeed the beginning of their life together.

The Job

"Hurry up!" Chloe, already shivering under several layers of clothing and blankets, said, "Get another piece of wood."

"Take a deep breath, sweetheart. Cooper told her that the fire was still burning brightly. "We have no idea how long the blackout will last, so we must preserve our wood."

"Says the man who gets the newspaper in a tank top outside."

He retorted, "Who also happens to be the same guy who spent four days camping in a blizzard when he was nine." "Believe me, Chloe. I know how to deal with it."

His preparations for an intimate evening with his lover had already been derailed. Chloe arrived home three hours ago after working an extra-long shift as a pharmacist at a downtown hospital. He'd been waiting for her, ready to preheat the oven and prepare salmon with sweet potatoes for her. It was her favorite meal, and he was hoping for a romantic Friday evening with her.

He was aware that a storm was approaching, but he didn't give it much thought. He was more prepared than anyone, having grown up in Minnesota and seeing more than his fair share of blizzards. Then the power went out before he could even switch on the oven, and their romantic evening was ruined.

He could tell Chloe wasn't in the mood for romance. Having spent her whole life in South Florida. That was evident from the fact that she wore too many layers just to get to work. This was her first big blizzard, and she wasn't having a good time with it so far.

“Oh, my God!” How can anyone manage to stay alive amid this nonsense?” Chloe sighed. “When I moved here last spring, I knew I'd have to adapt, just not like this!”

“You get used to it,” Cooper said as he hugged her even tighter.

She said, "Not soon enough for a Florida baby." “It wasn't until I was 22 years old that I saw snow for the first time.”

“I confess that the excitement wears off fast, but you get used to it. You've also grown to like it.”

“No disrespect to your hometown of Connecticut, but I'd rather be on South Beach in my bikini right now.”

"None taken," he said. "I appreciate your sentiments, Dave, but I'd rather concentrate on staying alive. In this kind of cold, there's just so much I can pretend."

She shivered again as she rubbed her hands together. She sounded almost panicked as if the storm and outage would last forever. Cooper couldn't think of anything else he could do for his lover. Knowing she was uncomfortable and upset was not a fun sensation.

He continued to try to warm her up by holding her tightly and stoking the fire in the fireplace that he'd been keeping burning for many hours. For both of them, it was an unfamiliar situation, and not only because of the weather.

While gazing at the flames, he said, "I'm sorry, Chloe." "Believe me when I say that this is not how I intended to spend my evening."

"Cooper, I believe you. Even, don't apologize," Chloe advised. "I should be the one apologizing. Since the power went out, I've been a pain in the neck."

"I'd say you don't have to apologize, but I'm not good at lying to you, so I won't."

"I appreciate that," she said dryly. "I just... I don't like feeling like this. We were without electricity for three days after a hurricane

passed through my neighborhood when I was eight years old. I recall my younger brother whining at every goddamn hour, but I held my ground. I even assisted my father in cleaning up the yard."

"To be honest, you can do it in a bikini as well."

"But that isn't the issue. What bothers me is that I've been in difficult circumstances before, whether it was blackouts, disasters, or a hospital meningitis outbreak. I've always managed to persevere, adapt, and remain resilient. But now... with this storm and all this cold... I feel so pitiful."

"Why?" you may wonder. In a blizzard-induced outage, there's only so much you can do."

"Damn it, I know! I just feel like I'm capable of more... especially when I'm with the man I care about."

Cooper's heart pounded a little faster. He glanced over at his shivering lover and forgot about the cold and the storm for a brief moment. This was the first time it felt sincere... that she really cared for him, even in such trying circumstances.

He wasn't sure whether she realized how serious what she'd just said was. That may have been a serious symptom of the cold playing with

her mind, for all he knew. His gut told him she meant it when he looked at her. That meant he needed to put in more effort.

With a renewed sense of purpose, Cooper devised a new strategy for demonstrating his love for Chloe. It wasn't enough to cook her a delicious meal on a Friday night. He wanted to make a bold gesture even in a darkened townhouse in the middle of a blizzard with just a finite supply of firewood. As he drew his lover closer, he devised a new strategy.

“You've improved, Chloe. He told her, "You're better than any woman I’ve ever met."

“That's thoughtful of you, Cooper,” she said, “but it doesn't make me any less pitiful.”

“Frustration is not the same as helplessness. They're not the same thing under any circumstance. You're helpless because you've used all of your choices and there's nothing else you can do. Frustration indicates that you can try a little harder than you wish you had.”

“The electricity is still out, the heater is broken, and we've already consumed the majority of what we can't microwave. “Because there's one option, we haven't tried... one that I don't believe would be acceptable in the circumstances.”

"Oh?" says the speaker." Chloe inquired, puzzled. "Can you tell me which one it is?"

Cooper smiled at her with a confident yet seductive grin. He typically gave her the look when he had something unexpected or tempting in store for her. That kind of thing typically necessitated a lot of forethought on his part. He intended to wing it this time, though.

He let go of her without saying something and got up to get another piece of firewood from the rack next to their fireplace. He made sure to get a large one that would burn for a long time without requiring much stoking. He needed the time for reasons that his lover would soon discover.

He turned around to face his lover after putting it on the fire and making it burn for a while. He then stripped down to his briefs, which must have seemed foolish given their current situation.

"As much as I enjoy watching you flaunt those manly muscles," Chloe said, puzzled but fascinated, "I'm always inclined to point out the danger here," she added.

“I understand. “I’m ready to take a chance,” he said, confidently standing before her in nothing but a pair of black boxers. “A man does it for the woman he loves.”

Those fateful words reverberated throughout the room. He could see it in her eyes. He sought to imitate her tone in order to convey his seriousness. He genuinely cared for her, to the point that he would endure the cold for her. She got the message loud and clear if the way her eyes swept down his half-naked body was any indicator.

He added, "Stop me if my timing is off or if my idea is dumb."

“From where I’m sitting, it's looking less and less dumb by the second,” Chloe grumbled.

“Then I won't have to be too harsh when I tell you, Chloe, that there's a more powerful way to keep you warm...

a method that can demonstrate your worth in the face of any adversity. I’ll be there to keep you warm whether it's sunny, cold, snowy, or dark.”

Cooper was more determined than he'd ever been in his adult life when he talked. He knelt down and crawled into his girlfriend's grasp as the freezing air blew through his blacked-out townhouse. She opened up the covers she'd clung to so tightly and welcomed

him into her embrace in a gesture that showed how much she desired his warmth.

He then kissed her passionately on the mouth, allowing the heat from his body to blend with hers, with only the glowing light of the fire lighting their surroundings. Even though she was still wearing several layers of clothes, the heat was more significant than the flames. Cooper's gesture took on a new significance as a result of this.

Chloe exclaimed, "Cooper... so wet."

He claimed, "I can make you warmer."

"I believe you," she said. “Tell me, though... does it need me to remove my clothing?”

“Well, if you want to get the most out of the effects...”

Cooper didn't even get to finish his sentence. Chloe was already eagerly removing the various layers of clothing she'd hurriedly put on after the power went out, so he didn't have to. He also assisted her in getting out of her sweatpants by taking her sweater off over her head.

They stayed under the covers, which made it a little clumsy and noisy. Her undershirt became entangled at one stage, and he had to

assist her in removing it. They ended up laughing and fumbling under the covers until she was barefoot. Cooper made it a point to take her in his embrace as soon as her flesh was revealed, his skin making contact with hers. A special kind of warmth emanated from that touch.

"Oh Cooper," she sighed, her hands sticking to his skin with zeal.

He smiled as she touched him, her large breasts pushing up against his stomach. The feeling of her smooth womanly flesh rubbing up against his had always been one of his favorites. They'd never had such a strong desire to get to know each other. Cooper got right to work making the best of the situation.

He wrapped their naked bodies in the thick blankets they'd borrowed from their bed, laying her down on the carpet with the raging fire just a few feet away. He kissed her once more after that. He added some extra touching this time, feeling up her womanly body and building up extra heat in the process.

From the way he caressed her face to the way he fondled her breasts, he touched her with extra affection and energy. Chloe had always loved that kind of concentrated and intimate foreplay. The fact that it provided real warmth was an added bonus.

But the warmth grew rapidly, to the point that simply touching and kissing wasn't enough. Cooper felt a growing erection in his boxers as he caressed his lover under the covers. He hadn't expected his attempts to be as successful as they were, given how cold it was. He took advantage of the situation as well, pressing his hardened bulge against his lover's inner thigh.

“Wow! Is that another of those effects, I'm getting the impression?” Chloe made a sly remark.

“It depends,” Cooper quips jokingly. “How do you think you'd react if I said yes?”

“These panties can't fall off quickly enough!”

That was all Cooper needed in terms of confirmation. He removed his boxers and assisted Chloe out of her underwear with a confident smile and a burning determination.

He rekindled their intimate touching now that he was fully naked under the thick blankets. There were no roadblocks this time. It was just her and his body, bare and exposed, relying on each other for warmth. Everything about it seemed so right, not to mention enticing.

Cooper felt his lover's arousal match him as their flesh met and shared warmth. Her body's warmth turned into a full-fledged heat, particularly between her legs. He put himself between Chloe's lets, drawn to the heat as any sane man would in such cold. She eagerly welcomed him once more. He joined her inside the embrace.

"Oh, Cooper!" She let out a gasp.

"Chloe..." he exclaimed; his face flushed with emotion.

The act of holding his girlfriend warmly morphed into making love to her at that precise moment. Cooper kissed her again, their bodies now entwined. They started moving together, their hard manly flesh rubbing up against the hot womanly depths. It wasn't the kind of sex they usually had while they were having fun. This was a passionate act that also happened to provide some much-needed warmth.

Cooper made love to his girlfriend with the attitude that he was doing more than just proving his honesty, fueled by the warmth and the passion that drove it. He was holding her safe and shielding her from the bitter cold. There was never a more compelling reason for a man to love his girlfriend in all the respects she deserved.

He took his time, keeping a steady yet enthusiastic pace. His body moved under the covers in response to their mutual desires,

exchanging deep kisses and passionate touching along the way. Such powerful efforts were so successful, Cooper said, that they made him sweat. That was an achievement in and of itself, but hearing his lover moan in gleeful ecstasy was even more rewarding.

“Cooper...

In such emotion, she said, "I love you."

He said to her without hesitation, "I love you too."

There was no room for doubt. It felt so genuine, given the circumstances of their situation. There could be no more doubt if he and Chloe could confess their love during a storm after all of their intricate plans had failed. He adored her, and she reciprocated his feelings.

He and Chloe slept together for as long as their frail bodies would allow. Chloe had cried out with that particular euphoric moan on many occasions, hinting that she had reached that special peak. He became engrossed in the ecstasy as well, finally hitting his limit. They were both exhausted by that point, having spent so much time and effort building the warmth that would shield them from the cold and other dangers.

They stayed curled up in each other's embrace, sharing both warmth and desire, even after the lovemaking had ended. Even as the fire in the fireplace dwindled in size, Chloe was no longer shivering. That gave him confidence that his efforts had paid off. He'd done exactly what he'd said he'd do: he'd kept his lover warm.

For the rest of the night, he was content to lie naked with her under the covers, holding each other warm before the sun rose. Then, after what must have been fate's prank, the power was restored. Although it was reassuring, it was also startling, and neither of them was prepared for the moment to end.

"What's up, Logan?" Chloe, who was still curled up next to him, said.

"Yes, darling?" he asked, a loving smile on his face.

"Would you mind turning off the lights while I add another log to the fire?"

Dancing in the Rain

Eleanor Maxwell's life was not going as she had planned. It had been three years since we had seen each other. Over those years, she and her husband Juan fought often, with Juan telling her that she would never amount to anything. Her cheeks were always stained with tears as she would often look in the mirror at the end of the day and insist, she was just where she should be. Nothing had been said to her to the contrary.

Eleanor's world came crashing down a few months after she left her home when she walked in on her husband and his mistress. All she could do was stand there, fighting the desire to throttle them both. She refused to let her tears fall, even though they were welling up in her eyes once more, as they always did. She had no intention of providing this man with the pleasure of seeing that. The room was deafeningly quiet as if time had stopped. And the hands on the clock above the stove were frozen in place. As she stood outside on their porch, the last words spoken before the door clicked were still ringing through her ears.

"You have the upper hand." Those two words crushed all hopes she had for a happy life. With those two sentences, their plans for raising children and building a house were shattered. Eleanor walked down the stairs and into the night with a heavy sigh, not wanting to look back and see if one of them had come outside or was staring out the window at her. She made the decision to walk away with her head raised as high as she could.

The wedding passed them by, and the young couple was on their own before they knew it. Right in front of them is the real world. That's when their love was put to the ultimate test. Many days were packed with both working and never really seeing each other. Their schedules never seemed to match since she worked at a clothes store, and he worked at a machine shop. Eleanor wished she didn't have to work some days so she could spend more time with him, but that wasn't going to happen. Throughout it all, it didn't seem that something was wrong. Why couldn't two young people face the same obstacles regularly and overcome them? Isn't it true that they adored each other?

One day after their third anniversary, the cracks began to appear. Eleanor sensed the tension in the hotel room and didn't feel as connected to her as she had in the past. The then-young wife was

constantly checking in with her husband to see if something was wrong or if he was still pleased with her. The answer was always the same:

“Of course, I’m fine.” She didn't want to question it when she was asked, but it was something that was always bothering her. Was he really pleased, or did he feel compelled to say so? He didn't hold her in the same way he used to. Conversations, on the other hand, never seemed to go as far. She yearned for a closer relationship with him and would go to any length to make him happy. In a last-ditch effort, she agreed to a divorce. It ripped her heart in two, but she decided it was worth it if this small break made him feel closer to her in the end. She didn't want him to feel confined in any way.

After some time had passed, Eleanor received the phone call she had been anticipating.

“Hello, Eleanor.” It's Juan here. I was hoping to see if you wanted me to pick you up after work. I’ve decided it's time for me to return home.”

Eleanor's heart swelled with delight as he finished his sentence. He yearned to return home! Of course, she decided, and he did indeed return to her. You'd think that was the end of it. They would reunite,

love would triumph above everything, and they would live happily ever after. But it didn't turn out that way. Love isn't something that happens and then vanishes. For a while, after Juan returned, everything seemed to be fine. Eleanor did everything she could to make him happy after they forgave each other. Perhaps that was the problem. She disliked confrontations with him and always caved in because she didn't want him to leave.

If only that was all she had to do to hold her husband around. Months passed, and things appeared to be looking up for the Maxwells. Eleanor was ecstatic because Juan was beginning to pay more attention to her. She had finally made him feel like she was the only woman in his life.

Things didn't last long, though. The petty battles erupted again before Eleanor's eyes. Something was bothering her, and she began to suspect that something wasn't quite right. It seemed to persist no matter how hard she tried to drive them away.

A few weeks later, the snowball effect began. Then there was the photograph she discovered in his top drawer. It seemed innocent at first, but Eleanor knew it wasn't. The pictures were intended for her, Juan would say. She'd rip them up and throw them at him in a fit of rage, knowing it wasn't true. He seemed to be physically and

mentally withdrawing as well. On her days off, he would always make an explanation for why he didn't want to be at home. He'd say he didn't want to be at home with her because he didn't feel like it. This tore at her heart until she could no longer bear it.

She worked up the courage to inquire if he really loved her. Eleanor wanted to see the guy she had Maxwell in love with when they were both teenagers by looking deep into his hazel eyes. He didn't seem to be there anymore. In his place was a guy who seemed to have forgotten about their past lives as well as their future plans. Eleanor searched desperately for a spark, but the silence assured her that there was none to be found.

"Listen, Eleanor, we've had too many problems in the last few months, with the war and the mistrust... it's just not working out." He spoke slowly and simply, avoiding eye contact.

"We were, however, figuring things out! Isn't it true that we wanted to try again? Have you been attempting? I've done everything I can to make you happy.

"It necessitates more. We can still be friends, but I'm done with this marriage. I don't need all of this anxiety."

"That's a lot of bull!! Eleanor blew up. She'd had enough of it. She couldn't contain her anger any longer.

"Who is she?"

"Can you tell me what you're talking about?"

"I'd like to know who it is because it's obvious you've moved on... probably well before the divorce."

"Eleanor, there is no one. There has simply been just too much drama for me, and I believe it is best that we part ways." He tried to put his hand on her shoulder, but she shook it off violently.

"Bull!" She spited once more before leaping from the couch to dash into the bedroom.

It had only been a few months since the blowout, but Eleanor remembered it like it was yesterday. The events of that night, on the other hand, were a blur. She ended up returning to live with her parents in order to clear her mind. When she returned to the apartment to find him refusing to leave, the temporary break turned into a permanent one. She had no idea what had caused him to change his mind, but she didn't want to fight any longer. Instead, she informed him she'd be by to pick up her belongings as soon as she could.

Eleanor had intended on going there the night she found out about his other girlfriend to try one more time to make things right. When she walked in on the two of them, their plans changed. That night, all she wanted to do was leave and not look back. How was he able to pull that off? How could he just squander a relationship like that?

Eleanor has gradually begun to feel better after many counseling sessions with her friends and several sleepless nights. She wasn't in the best of circumstances, but she knew she should carry on. This was put to the test one evening when she was out with her friends at one of their favorite restaurants.

"Did you hear that Juan and that woman he's shacking up with are expecting a child?"

Eleanor smiled a little bit as she processed the question, which seemed to come out of nowhere. The ladies who surrounded her were all curious as to what she was thinking...

"He's no longer able to harm me. That was the very last thing he could think about. I will no longer be harmed by him."

Eleanor couldn't stop laughing as the ladies chatted about their weekend plans. She had been through so much, and it felt as though

a huge weight had been lifted from her shoulders. She would be able to break free from the arrows that were being fired at her one by one. She could finally see that despite the battles, the affair, and the pregnancy, there was little else he could do to make her miserable. She was eventually able to move on and be happy.

Refusing to Let Go

Adam stood there watching raindrops cascade down the driver's side windshield. The small drops that started at the top gradually merged with other droplets, finally forming a single raindrop that traveled down the glass. His face lit up as he recalled the days of riding in the back seat of his parents' car, picking raindrops to win races down the windshield.

Adam leaned back in his seat and gazed out the window, past the raindrops to the tiny blue house on the corner. He watched as lights switched on and off in various windows, thinking Hannah was finishing up her preparations. As he stood, eyes closed, listening to the storm, memories filled Adam's mind. His favorite images were of Hannah sprinting to the car in her shorts and tank tops. In the summer, she was always the most involved. When he drove to her house to pick her up in the winter, it was usually the most amusing to watch. She could never make it to her car without falling on her sidewalk and then laughing at herself the rest of the night.

Adam checked the front door with his eyes open. Hannah is also missing. He shifted his gaze to the passenger seat, where he had stashed a few coffee cups. He was still enthralled by the sight of her sitting there. She is the quietest person Adam knows when she is with other people, but when she sits in that seat, she might talk for hours. It wouldn't be the same without him. Adam turned around to see Hannah shut the door and walk towards the car, which he had seen out of the corner of his eye. As she took short measures with her arms crossed at her chest, her body appeared rigid. Adam reached across the car to the passenger door and pushed it open, concerned. Hannah slipped inside without making eye contact.

"Hey, are you all, right?" Adam was the one who inquired.

"Can we just go for a drive for a little while?" Hannah asked softly. Adam locked his gaze on her for a few moments as she sat motionless in her seat. Finally, he grinned and sped away down the highway.

For what felt like an eternity, the two remained in silence. Adam couldn't decipher what she was doing. Her arms were still crossed and her body was clenched. She kept an eye out the window and sniffed every five minutes or so. Adam knelt down beside her and rested his hand on her leg. "You know, you should speak to me," he

said. "We haven't been together for four years and you somehow don't tell me when something is wrong."

Tears streamed down her face as she turned to face Adam. "We're on our way." As she buried her face in her hands, her sniffs turned into sobs. Adam stood there watching as one of the powerful women he'd come to know crumbled in the seat next to him. He immediately stopped the car and took a deep breath, pondering what he should say next.

As he rubbed her back, he asked, "Where to?" Adam leaned back, knowing he'd asked the wrong question as her sobs became more intense. Hannah dried the mascara smeared under her eyes and held her breath as she calmed down.

She continued to sniffle as she said, "California."

Adam's heart sunk, and he was filled with doubts. "My father was offered a fantastic job there. I suppose it's a quiet neighborhood. And my mother said we could get a dog if we wanted one," she added, fighting back tears. That was the Hannah Adam was familiar with. She tried to be optimistic even in the worst of circumstances. He let out a sigh. He wondered if he would be able to survive without her. Adam looked for answers. He returned his gaze to the droplets

outside the glass. He saw a group of people forming and moving down the window, rolling out of the vehicle. In his mind, an idea developed slowly. They had to be in the same place at the same time. There was no other option. They had no choice but to do whatever they could to make it work.

Adam turned to face Hannah and said, "Marry me." Her sobbing ceased, and the car fell silent once more.

“What?” she asked quietly.

“Will you marry me, Hannah?”

As she held her breath, her eyes grew larger. She reclined in her seat; her hands folded in her lap. Adam was unconcerned about the silence. He wanted her to think about it. It was a significant option. While she turned to face him, he saw her eyes light up.

“Yes,” she said, her grin the biggest he'd ever seen. As he reached over and hugged her, Adam couldn't help but laugh with relief. He held her in his arms as she burrowed her face into his chest and laughed through her tears. He smiled as he took another look around his vehicle. The sound of rain was soothing and comforting. He squeezed Hannah's hand, clinging to the love of his life.

Eternal Flame

As requested, I pull up to the wooded, snowy driveway and park along the side of the road. When I look in the mirror, my mind wanders over my pale, simple 45-year-old face, hoping for the best, a fresh start. After texting him that "I'm here," I look around and wait patiently.

I see a very thin middle-aged man walking briskly up the driveway through the darkness and snow towards the vehicle a few minutes later. I leap out of my skin, nearly slipping on the ice. As I regain my composure, I walk over to meet him just as he approaches my car. He reaches in and extends his arms to embrace me. "Hello, I'm glad you could make it; I wasn't sure if you'd turn up with the weather and everything."

I take a step forward and embrace the hug, his powerful arms wrapping around me, and I close my eyes for a brief moment. I feel at ease, and that realization hits me like a ton of bricks. He lets go of my hand and extends a friendly hand to me. We cautiously walk down the icy road towards his building, and I put mine in his.

"There's no problem. I'm just looking forward to seeing you again after such a long time."

"I can't believe you really showed up. I'm embarrassed to admit how many times a woman has said she was going to meet me and then failed to turn up. I have a pair of low-hanging apple trees in the driveway that has ripped my antenna off on many occasions. That's something I didn't want to happen to you."

I keep a close eye on my steps, so I don't trip, and I pay attention to everything he says. I start to blush when I catch a glimpse of his beautiful blue eyes, which send shivers down my spine and make my heart skip a beat. Before he notices that I am looking at him, I quickly turn away and look down at my feet.

"OK, that's fine. I noticed it was narrow and assumed you were being careful. All is fine." I smile and keep my eyes peeled for risk.

As we arrive at his front entrance, he assists me in climbing the steps and then unlocks the door for me. I get a little giddy when I walk in because he turns around and gives me a huge bear hug. "See, I told you I like to embrace, and I'll finally show you all of my various hugs. My big bear hugs were always a hit with the kids."

His arms encircle my body, but he is gentle with me once more. before releasing me and motioning for me to take a seat next to him in a chair. I take off my coat and hang it on the back of the chair behind me, still unsure of what to do. We chat for hours about education, growing up, old friends, and events from the last twenty years or so.

The next thing I know, he's looking at me, and I'm blushing uncontrollably. When he watches one of his kittens nestle itself right between my breasts in my low v neck tight-fitting sweater, the room becomes silent. His tongue darts in and out along his lower and then upper lip, easily moistening his lips. I keep a close eye on him and then quickly look away when I realize he's captured me. His hunger-filled eyes dart across my face and then down my body.

When I smile at him, he clears his throat and looks shocked. I know he wants me because I read him like a book, even though I just came to talk to a high school classmate and make a good friend. Apparently, he had other plans all along, or our chemistry was too intense for us to combat because I've had the feeling that we were meant to be together since the moment we touched and he took my hand.

I begin to feel a deep ache inside of me that grows worse with each passing minute, so I shift in my seat in an attempt to relieve it. "So, when did your divorce become final?" he asks quietly.

"Two months ago, even though I filed the first part of April," I tell him as the painful memories resurface. When minor children are involved, it takes 6 months to have one in Michigan, so I'll have to stay where I am until they turn 18. Even if I wanted to, I couldn't move."

"Oh, no. That's how I remember it. When I got divorced and eventually got custody of the kids, I was overjoyed, but I quickly discovered how difficult it was to deal with my ex-wife."

"Please accept my heartfelt apologies. I'm just relieved you received them."

After my stomach begins to growl, I check my watch and see that I've been here for three hours. "How in the world did this happen? I can't believe I've been talking to you for the past three hours and haven't realized it. I suppose it's just because I'm so at ease with you. It's as if we've known each other for years."

I stand up, signaling that I'm going, and he laughs. He appears in front of me in the blink of an eye and then takes me into his embrace.

His solid, warm arms encircle me once more in a caring or welcoming, embrace. Maybe it's just my imagination, but I swear he's holding me for longer than he should.

It thrills me to get a whiff of his raw masculinity. My senses perk up as my body tells me loud and clear that I want him. He proves to me that he is capable of carrying me to the bedroom by lifting me up. He just holds me up for a few seconds before letting me down.

"I see you're packing your belongings and getting ready to leave. Will you be able to drive this late? If you want to visit, I can always let you sleep in my room while I sleep on the couch."

"No, I'm fine. I need to return before the kids become enraged. I told them I'd be back before ten o'clock, and I'll be back about twelve." As I begin to put on my coat and walk to the entrance, I laugh.

He arrives ahead of me and leaves the door open for me as he puts his shoes on. "I'll take you back so you don't hurt yourself. This driveway is very slick. I'm the one with the flashlight, after all." When I pass through the doorway and past his hungry gaze, he smiles.

He takes my hand and walks me down the steps to the driveway. "When do you think you'll be able to see me again?" He patiently awaits my answer.

"Well, I'll leave you a message when I get home, and hopefully I'll be able to come up here and see you again soon." I'm very interested in meeting your youngest sibling. Maybe my kids and yours will have a good time when the park opens in the spring." I smile and look at him, secretly hoping he will decide on staying the night and end up in bed with me. But he doesn't, and I'm left sitting in my car in the freezing cold, watching him cautiously return to his home.

I stare at myself in the mirror once more, cursing myself for not staying. Every fiber of my being tells me to stay and see if what I'm feeling is true. Finally, I exhale deeply and drive away. I return home, hopeful for the future, to find my three children sleeping in the living room, waiting for me. After leaving a message for him, I let them stay and sleep in the chair next to them so that when they wake up, they can see that I arrived safely.

When I wake up in the morning, my seventeen-year-old daughter sits next to me, waiting for me to say something. I open my eyes just wide enough to feel the chill in the air. "I apologize. I got home about twelve o'clock. We had a lot to catch up on and just so much time. I

checked my watch and saw that it had been three hours, so I rushed up and returned home. I couldn't wake you up because you were still sleeping, so I couldn't tell you I was home. Instead, I reasoned that if I slept in the chair, you'd notice me the moment you awoke."

"I can't believe you didn't just spend the night. It was something I was half expecting. After all, we both know it wasn't a date as you claimed."

"Pardon me, young lady. I went up there to pay a visit to an old classmate and nothing else. He isn't my boyfriend; in fact, he is just a friend."

"All right, whatever. In any case, I am not bothered. I am so happy you're back; the twins were yelling at each other and making me insane. I was on the verge of strangling them." She gives me a sidelong glance before heading upstairs to her place.

I look down to see a message from him after hearing a ding on my phone. "Hey, I was hoping to see if we could all get together at your house this weekend? My daughter is desperate to meet you all because she is lonely out here in the middle of nowhere."

"To be honest, I don't know yet. I'm not sure when their father will receive them. I won't know until later this week, but there's something I need to tell you. I know you'll think I'm nuts, but I can't seem to get you out of my head. I haven't been able to stop thinking about how you sound, smell, and your voice and smile since I first saw you and you hugged me. When you first hugged me, I felt like I was home."

There was no answer. I keep waiting and waiting. There's nothing. I see words all of a sudden.

" I share your sentiments. I just didn't want to scare you away by telling you. The way I feel about you terrifies me. I don't understand it, but I feel like my soulmate. I can't believe we squandered twenty-plus years."

"I am so happy that you feel the same way. I was convinced I was going crazy. I'm in love with you and want you to move in with us in some way. I'm not sure how or when, but I'm not going to be able to live without you. I understand it's difficult, but I need your presence in my life."

I share your sentiments. I'm just not sure how it'll go with the kids. I believe they should meet my youngest and see how they get along

because if they don't and she doesn't like you, we won't be able to proceed. My first responsibility is to my children; what I want doesn't matter."

My heart begins to hurt as soon as I hear those words. When the Bangles' Eternal Flame comes on the radio, I sing my heart out. That is the title of our album. We both enjoy it, and that is exactly how I feel about him. I just hope his little one gets along with my three. All the love in the world won't make a difference if this isn't the case.

My heart begins to ache once more as I remember that I may have just fallen in love with the love of my life and had to let it go. I make breakfast for the twins and hope that it will be so much simpler. I take a shower and call him after they've all gone to their quarters.

" I need to speak with you again."

"I have to work tonight, love, so I'll see you tomorrow." I pick up my daughter from my mother in the morning, and it would be great if you could meet her. Before we go any further, I believe it is a good idea to do so. Then, if she likes you, I'll be able to meet your children."

"All right. If she likes me, can I spend the night tomorrow? I'm free for the next two days because my ex has the kids."

"We'll see, honey. If you linger, I'll have to return her to her mother because I don't want her to hear us making love. That's just not something I do, and I have no idea how loud you are."

"All right. I see your point. So, when you wake up tomorrow morning, let me know what you think. I'll be ready when you are."

"Sure love, believe me when I say I want you. I haven't had sex in a long time, and I'd like to make you some crazy passionate love. I want you to feel the same way I do about you."

" Baby, you have no idea how much I adore you or how much I would go out of my way for you. I can't believe we've only just met again, and I've already fallen in love with you. It's incredible."

"Honey, I've got to get up and get ready for work." When I get home, I'll call you. I will always love you. You are my everlasting flame. It's just about me. Keep that in mind at all times, even if things don't work out."

I hesitate, unsure of what to say. I take a deep breath in and say, "I love you, baby," as I sit there. Have a wonderful day, and I hope to hear from you in the morning. "Until then."

He hangs up, and I just look at the phone silently. Even though every minute is packed with memories of last night, I clean up the house and try not to think about him for the rest of the day. Finally, I fall asleep on the couch at the end of the day.

The next morning, his voice wakes me up on the phone. "Honey, she expresses a strong desire to meet you. "Will 2 p.m. suffice?"

I rise and take a few moments to clear my mind. "Yes, without a doubt. Since the kids are going to their father's this morning, I'll have plenty of time to get there. Is there something I can bring?

"No way. Just your lovely self. I have to go, but I'll see you at my house at 2 p.m. I'm in love with you. Then we'll talk. Goodbye."

"Goodbye."

I shower and drop the kids off at their father's house before heading up to see him. He moves in with his daughter the next thing I know, and then we marry.

I'm looking back on the first day now, twenty years later. I have a soft smile on my face as I recall the first time he took my hand, and then I begin to weep as Eternal Flame plays on the radio, and I realize

he is no longer with us. I'm just glad that the years we spent together were the best of our lives.

Conclusion

This compilation of tales is just what the doctor ordered. While these stories are not romantic in nature, they each have a happy ending and are inspirations to embrace love in your life. The stories are short and sweet; they are perfect for bedtime. The best of these tales include positive messages about true love, true friendship, and the power of the human spirit. Enjoy!

Love is a wonderful thing. It can help make us feel alive even when we are in pain or when we feel hopeless about ourselves. But finding love can be a daunting task for many people who have been hurt in various ways, yet still want to find it again. So many people have lost their heartbreak to some unrequited feelings for someone they don't really know well enough or understand well enough to love well enough and just end up wanting something better without ever being able to get it or realizing what they could have had instead. That's why we have stories where love doesn't just happen by chance or happen by fate, but rather is something that you have to make happen. Love is a choice, not a feeling, and if you feel paralyzed by

your feelings and unable to act on them because you worry that it would be selfish of you or self-centered, then you need to remind yourself that love and loving someone have nothing to do with your selfishness... it has only got to do with being good to another person who deserves your love. And sometimes the best way to prove how much you love someone is by giving them what they deserve: You! and if you let someone else's needs guarantee your existence in their life, then you're just wasting your time because, in the end, they aren't going to care about you as much as you care about them. And if you commit to loving someone, then be willing to set them free and let them be happy with someone who deserves their love. Love is a deep emotion that people choose to feel for others when they meet those special people in their lives. Love can be a feeling that goes beyond a simple friendship, but it's more than that too; love is something effortless and a way of life. Love can fill any void in one's heart and soul.

There's nothing like an intense, first-person account of someone being stabbed or shot or chemotherapy to make me think about how great my life is.

These stories will take you through some difficult times with characters that you'll come to care about and root for. We hope after

reading these heartfelt tales, you'll be able to find the courage to live your own fascinating story. In addition to making, you think more deeply about your life, these stories will make you look at others around you in a new light and will even have you believe that there's someone for everyone.